C000171889

THE
CONTROLLED

WRITTEN BY

P.J. WILLETT

MONTAG

First Montag Press E-Book and Paperback Original Edition June 2022

Copyright © 2022 by P.J. Willett

As the writer and creator of this story, P.J. Willett asserts the right to be identified as the author of this book.

All rights reserved. No part of this book may be reproduced or transmitted in any form or by any means, electronic or mechanical, including photocopying, recording, or by any information storage and retrieval system without the written permission of the author, except where permitted by law. However, the physical paper book may, by way of trade or otherwise, be lent, re-sold, or hired out without the publisher's prior consent.

Montag Press ISBN: 978-1-957010-11-3
Design © 2022 Amit Dey

Montag Press Team:

Cover Illustration: myriax
Photographer: Simon Crowther
Editor: John Rak
Managing Director: Charlie Franco

A Montag Press Book
www.montagpress.com
Montag Press
777 Morton Street, Unit B
San Francisco CA 94129 USA

Montag Press, the burning book with the hatchet cover, the skewed word mark and the portrayal of the long-suffering fireman mascot are trademarks of Montag Press.

Printed & Digitally Originated in the United States of America
10 9 8 7 6 5 4 3 2 1

This book is a work of fiction. Names, characters, places, and incidents are either products of the author's vivid and sometimes disturbing imagination or are used fictitiously without any regards with possible parallel realities. Any resemblance to actual persons, living or dead, events, or locales is entirely coincidental.

BLURBS

Willett comes in the tradition of JG Ballard: nightmarish, a bleak warning, yet filled with humanity. One of the best, most assured debut novels I've read in some time.

John Niven

Detail by terrifying detail, *The Controlled* slowly reveals a violent, dark, and gritty near-future dystopia. Focused up close-and-personal on a group of students and educators, these very real, very flawed people's stories, vibrantly rendered and true to life, are a horror show of systemic injustice and class exploitation. Strong emotional responses pull the reader in, to root for many characters and despise others. A thoroughly engaging book.

Kathy L. Brown,
author of *The Big Cinch*

Fast paced and disturbing in the kind of way that makes you want to flip to the next page as quickly as possible, P.J. Willett's *The Controlled* tells the story of what happens when a system of authority under the guise of education attempts to take over not just the minds, but the bodies of students deemed out of control, who are known as SUBS. The result is a gripping tale of brutal consequences to the deserved and undeserved alike. Bookended by a clever and original beginning and ending chapter, this is a great book for fans of dystopian stories that revolve around Orwellian appetites for power.

Jonathan R. Rose,
author of *Carrion*,
The Spirit of Laughter and *Gato Y Lobo*.

DEDICATION

A huge thank you to:

My favourites for your names.
NL, JB, & JR for your clarity.
FCH&S for *everything*.
Those lacking Grace for the lesson in hypocrisy.

ACKNOWLEDGMENTS

My favourites - with your permission, I took your names. I needed to reference all of you but the characters were entirely incidental (although Zach Goggins is pretty spot on – what a loser!) You were all the reason why teaching can be incredible. You are the inspiration behind this book's main message – *everyone* deserves the best education.

Natalie Leeson, you are, and will always be, the most incredible sufferer of first drafts. Without you, *all* my ideas would wither. You take my unique approach to grammar and unending sentences, and somehow know exactly what I want to say.

Justin Banks, I needed someone kind enough to be careful with me but honest enough to be cruel. There is no one better. Thank you for helping me know what to think about my book.

John Rak, when I had convinced myself there was nothing more to do, you came along. I have never enjoyed criticism as much. You turned The Controlled into what it is.

Montag & Charlie, you made this possible, thank you.

Kris & Fred, The Controlled was written when I was almost broken, thank you for keeping me together.

Harrison, Cooper, and Fletcher, you slowed my progress, considerably. You are the reason I didn't give up.

Sarah, my beaut, while I did this, you did *everything* else. I cannot wait until the day I can treat you to all that you deserve. I'm not sure it's possible to get there, but I'll keep doing the little I can because I know you'll keep doing everything else.

TABLE OF CONTENTS

1 – Clucky 1

2 – Tom Brown 4

3 – "The damage is done" 21

4 – Dean Sandler 29

5 – "You are not taking me with you" 46

6 – Sophie Burns 58

7 – "Under control" 71

8 – Zachary Noblie-Goggins 88

9 – "You have to fix this" 102

10 – Lauren Tamar 114

11 – "For his own good" 126

12 – Dickie Vaneman 142

13 – "We're fodder" 157

14 – Bradley Sherrington 168

15 – "High and mighty" 177

16 – "It's too late" 186

17 – Sally Simons. 193

18 – "No use complaining" 201

19 – "Still red". 207

20 – Mr. Drexler 216

21 – Dean Sandler 226

22 – Edmund Stanley. 237

23 – Bruno. 241

Author Bio. 244

1

CLUCKY

Clucky was incapable of anticipating the impending demise of her miserable existence. She panicked at the flapping, the shouting, and the smell of warm death. But Clucky did not savour these sights and sounds in the knowledge that they would be her last, because Clucky is a chicken.

She had been slung into a crate with sixty others the night before, packed and piled so tight their broken wings poked through the gaps. The crate had been stacked into the back of a truck and driven with a hundred other trucks in a snaking line, away from the old northern city that had been converted into a mega-farm (along with all the other repurposed cities) following the Corporate Conflict.

She had been kicked into a dust field amongst the thousands of pecking heads, an undulating sea of feathers and haze. A suited man had squealed in distress when he'd accidentally dropped his Block over the fence, grabbing a nearby Joe and casting him into the poultry to go fetch.

She had been corralled through a stainless-steel warehouse adorned with 'Work Harder!' posters where the conveyered sorting line separated the dead product - the choice chunks of breast and thigh, bleached of disease, and neatly packaged in Rego's Quaint Family Farm trays. The heads, skin, and feet, rammed into vats ready to be slurried up and boiled down into filler for food pouches.

She had been squeezed into a pen by Abdul, a boy glazed with indifference. Young enough that he should've been completing his final year of education, but, after a serious assault on a gentleman called Edmund Stanley, the General Manager of Site 97, had received early classification as a farming Joe.

And by morning she was hanging upside down, the juddering pull on her feet swaying her head from side to side, waiting for her manic flapping to be stilled by a circular spinning blade.

The slice was sudden, the steel gushing the throat in an instant. She felt the brief bubbling agony of boiling water before everything dulled to darkness. Then she was a carcass, to be defeathered, dismembered, and disembowelled.

Clucky had never entertained the notion that things should have been better, that the sheer miracle of her existence was deserving of reverence, that stars collapsed and atoms coalesced and myriad evolutions birthed multiple generations only for it all to end in the ignominy of being a fat kid's nuggets.

She wouldn't have been able to comprehend the forth-coming chaos signified by the indifferent boy leaning his head over the vat, his face a scrunched picture of pleading, before giving into his urge and biting off his bottom lip and letting a mouthful of tainted blood dribble in amongst the cheap chicken bits.

Clucky had accepted her wretched lot in life, right up until she was mushed into pink sludge, mixed with Abdul's bloodied drool and packaged into pouches to be sent to the zones. She lacked the capacity to understand, or the ability to alter, how awful everything was. She was a victim of the cheap desires of the intrinsically selfish.

Because Clucky was a chicken.

2

TOM BROWN

Tom had locked himself inside his home for more than half a year.

He'd been suspended from work seven months ago – escorted off-site by the General Manager's assistant ('his Janet'). She'd kept whispering sympathies and babbling about how embarrassed she was, how awful the accusation was, how everyone knew it wasn't true. But then she'd quickly ushered him out of the fire exit, away from the groups of kids roaming the corridors, obviously concerned he might try and molest a youngster on his way out. The rage and shame caused by the lie had waned after Tom's first month off. The constant crushing in his chest softened to a dull ache in his stomach. The sleepless anguish and aimless moping were replaced with a detached routine of daytime television and masturbation. Never venturing out of the house, as that made the nights come around too quickly, and the nights were too quiet for him to ignore the darkest thoughts still lurking behind the daytime distractions.

His work trousers were loose, so he slipped into his jeans and a polo shirt, giving a satisfied huff as he buckled his belt into a new hole. His weight loss was the one sorry victory he could pluck out of this whole farce.

The bathroom was cold and quiet, growing dimmer with each dying bulb. Replacing them was a small task, but it had been his wife's job, along with the thermostat, the food, the cleaning, and an endless list of other mysteries that constipated him with dread at the thought of trying to address. His disgrace had robbed him of the ability to convince her to stay, so he'd been alone in his bitter, dark home, eating cereal amidst the dust, ever since.

He offered a faint smile to his gaunt reflection before turning and dropping to his knees. He vomited his Rego-flakes neatly into the toilet bowl, brushed his teeth again, and picked up his empty backpack (he had nothing to fill it with – the only thing in his fridge was milk and old mustard). His head dizzied as he trudged down the stairs – the isolation had become a comfort; the thought of opening his front door made him want to weep.

Tom left his home for the first time in more than half a year.

It was an unimpressive house, miles from the village centre, on the outskirts, only a short walk to the zone. On a warm day, you could smell it – Zone 102. Different from the others only in number; miles of metal shutters and desolation, with pockets of towering Paradise Flats apartments, and rows of square wooden houses. At its centre, the Education Site, training the next generation of Joes and Janes – the occupations given to the boys and girls lucky enough to escape the Lines, but not competent enough to be Janets. A batch of them pressed their sardined faces against the windows of their grey bus as they were shipped to wherever their services were needed. Their tired gazes reminded Tom of the hopeless students he served.

As he took the familiar turns on his drive to work, the ritual unease returned, stronger than ever. A hopeless desire to freeze time and live in a world where the Sun comes up but his day never starts. The clock ticked on another minute and Tom kept driving. He had to. It was all he knew.

Tom had devoted more of his life to education than anything else. He had roamed every classroom and corridor of his site since long before it was even called a site, back when they were just 'schools' or 'academies.' As a teacher for twenty-five years, he'd talked at students for more hours than he had shared a bed with his wife (he'd done the calculation one day between the morning broadcast and his second joyless wank).

He thought about turning his car into a wall; if he crushed a leg, he wouldn't be able to return. That thought occupied him for the remainder of his journey.

He parked his car in the bay nearest the gate and got out without allowing himself time to consider driving away. The panic swirled his gut. His card swipe was met with a grating beep, so he pressed the reception button and waited. Hot saliva flooded his mouth, and he swallowed back the rushing urge to be sick again.

The buzzer crackled, then spoke, "You're early, Tom."

"Yes. I thought it might be... I thought... yes I am," he said.

"Stare at the camera."

After smiling at a small black box for an awkwardly long time, the gate unlocked with a clunk and rolled to one side. Tom walked through, but was stopped by another closed door, the main entrance. The building had changed since his banishment. The drab brick had been covered with bright plastic panels. A child's Duplo prison in an expanse of grass and concrete; its perimeter fence separating it from the cramped homes over which it cast its shadow. A huge logo hung above the entrance – Rego Ed: Site 102.

Tom learned that Rego was taking over during his first week of suspension. It wasn't a surprise – there had been rumours for a while, and they already controlled most of the other zoned sites across the Nation. The seizure was a swift process that had evolved from years of evading scrutiny.

Rego began as an electronics company, heralded for creating Blocks (small, transparent handheld computers). Despite functioning almost identically to every smart device that came before it, they were an instant necessity. Filling the palms to shepherd the lives of *everyone* who could find a way of affording it. After amassing more wealth than most countries, Rego diversified. Soon every shop, factory, and advert bore its logo – swathes of the workforce were 'downsized to exploit synergies' in its lauded pursuit of increased productivity. The plight of decimated communities lost in the fog of management soundbites and shareholder satisfaction. The promises of sunlit uplands for a reborn nation were broken. The unrest intensified into the Corporate Conflict and the Ministers begged the arsonists to put out the fires – Rego was given control of everything. There seemed to be a representative on one of the broadcasts at least once a week, informing the people of which public service was next in need of redemption. The demand to transfer its relentless excellence to the broken education system was inevitable. *Rego – always helping, always here.*

Tom had convinced himself his case would be poison to them – forget justice, he'd be culled at the first opportunity. But the months passed, and the sound of the flapping letter-box eventually stopped making him sick with fear. His notice never came. So, to prepare for his return, he read up on their 'pragmatic approach to redefining learning,' and watched broadcast clips of the CEO, Dickie Vaneman, announce rapid takeover after rapid takeover with the same thumbs-up, smiling promise to 'guarantee positive destinations for the clients of Zone… whatever.'

Despite Tom's instinctive hatred of everything Rego represented, his job mattered more than his principles – he was relieved they kept him on. Besides, how different could it be? He'd worked under enough regimes to expect the same misery, regardless of their promises. They *all* claim that whatever they bring is revolutionary, and whatever preceded them was shit. Tom was tired of being told how shit he was.

He shoved at the door but it didn't budge, so he pressed another reception button.

"What?!"

"Sorry... I'm still outside... there isn't a handle," he said.

"The camera, Tom. Always the camera."

"Oh... of course... sorry."

He looked into the camera again. This time the door opened after three green flashes. The recently appointed GM, Sophie Burns, was waiting in the hallway, the metal tip of her expensive shoe clacking as she tapped her toe.

"Good morning, Tom," she said. "We are pleased to have you back. Finally."

"Morning, Mrs. Burns."

"Please, unless clients are present, you may call me Sophie," she said. "I trust you understand how to use the doors from this point onwards, or is another demonstration required?"

"Nope... cameras... got it."

"Your image has been registered. You can gain entry to any room on the second, first, or ground floors. But I will need to escort you out of the building as the main doors remain locked during working hours. Understood?" she didn't wait for an answer. "Follow me."

All the old sights and sounds were hidden beneath a veneer. Everything was different. Staff portraits filled the reception walls, all posed so the beaming smiles angled up towards an oil painting of Dr. Vaneman. There were some new faces and lots of missing ones. The paint-chipped walls had been covered with floor-to-ceiling milky glass that scrolled electric words of inspiration. The stained carpet was now gleaming steel tiles. 'Generosity' flashed onto one of the glass walls and its purple reflection bounced through the corridor. Soft piano plinks echoed a piece of classical music – the type of unending tune that filled the void in a dentist's waiting area.

They walked by a darkened room. Peering in, Tom could see a man in a lab coat and a group of kids wearing Halos – chunky goggles that turned opaque and shone a band of light around the wearer's head when switched on; fancy pieces of kit that he and every other teacher had consigned to the cupboards because they had no clue how to use them, and no reason to learn.

"You'll be taking away an induction pack," Sophie said. "You will read it before tomorrow, but I'll fill you in on some details. The ground floor is now just for automated study sessions, mainly for Subs and Specials. The first floor is for Lows. The second floor, where you will facilitate, is for Mids. The third floor is for Tops only. It is Rego Ed policy that there is a much stricter adherence to client labelling, hence the floor separation," she stopped outside the entrance to the next room. "When you are issued with your Block, you won't need to keep peering into the cameras," she said, reaching into her pocket.

Tom tried to mask his excitement. Rego provided all their employees with the latest Blocks, he'd heard that the new editions could be unfolded until they were paper thin and metres wide – he couldn't wait to try one out, regardless of how distasteful the Rego corporation was. He was disappointed when Sophie's hand emerged empty. Confusion furrowed her brow as she patted her remaining pockets.

"… I'll just have to show you later," she said, opening the door by peering at the camera. The room blinked into life when she pressed a button on the wall. A large, friendly but featureless face filled the entire side of the room.

"Good morning, class," it spoke. "Know your duty. Do not refuse to do it. Let us begin."

"It is policy that all clients are permanently Haloed now," Sophie said. "All ground floor lessons are delivered through their headsets by this flawless facilitator. Never tired. Never unprepared. Never unprofessional."

"Never," Tom echoed.

The flawless facilitator looped back and repeated its message. Sophie pressed the button and the room went dark.

"Impressed?" she smiled.

"How many students are taught in this room?" Tom peered across what he'd worked out used to be the Sports Hall.

"Clients," Sophie corrected. "We call them clients. The answer is three hundred. With the six suites on the ground floor, we can cater for almost a third of our cohort."

"Six?" Tom said, picturing the old ground floor layout. "Two Dinner Halls, two Sports Halls, the Assembly Hall, and the Library? They're now giant classrooms?"

"Yes."

"Makes sense," Tom scoffed. "What do students need a library for anyway?"

"Our *clients* on the ground floor are Subs and Specials. What they *need* is consistency. All day, every day. More specific attention is only required as we climb the floors. It is policy that only the Tops have access to our outstanding teachers."

"Good for them," Tom said. He wanted to leave.

"Scepticism is a refuge for the weak, Tom," she said. "This works. Be onboard, or go elsewhere."

Tom had known Sophie before she was the GM, when she was just 'that bitch up in English' – she hadn't changed.

"No... it's just a lot to take in... I'm pleased to be back. I'd just like to have our... is it called bridge?" he said. She nodded. "Yeh, I'd just like to have our bridge meeting, get that out of the way, and then I can prepare for tomorrow."

"*Get that out of the way?*" she shook her head and blew out a deep sigh. "We don't get bridge meetings *out of the way*, Tom. They are a vital component of our revolutionary practice. I wasn't aware you were so busy. This meeting is important, but, if I'm keeping you from... *whatever* you've been filling your time with, feel free to leave."

"No. Sorry. You misunderstand," the tension from his first conversation in months clenched the sick lump in Tom's stomach. He thought about how he'd been filling his time, ghosting around in his pants, sobbing between documentary repeats. "I've... I've not been busy. I don't want to leave. I'm just anxious to get started."

"Fine. I'll show you your room first," she said, walking away.

The building had two huge wings jutting out from the central hub, with the East and West stairwells at the end of each. Sophie led Tom along the west wing and up to the second floor. She moved with such purpose that Tom needed to keep skipping into a light jog. She pointed at a black box out-side his old classroom. Tom stared into the camera and walked into his room after the door clicked. A wall knock-through meant it had doubled in size, and it had been gutted of all the trinkets he had collected during his career. The photos of past students, years of Thank You cards, a graffitied jumper covered in the messages from his favourite ever group. All of his memories were replaced with slick gloss walls and the empty smell of new paint. Everything he had was gone. He imagined his wife's voice insisting he stands up for himself, demanding his fury. But he no longer had to care about how disappointed he made her, so he shrugged and said nothing.

"The rest of your clients' desks will be in place for tomor-row," Sophie said. "You will position yourself in the centre of the room so that the seventy seats are arranged as policy demands." She pressed one of the white walls and it filled with the Rego logo. "You'll need to spend some time getting acquainted with your touchwall, otherwise you won't be able to provide the required experience tomorrow."

"Did you say seventy students!?" he said, dropping his backpack on a chair.

"*Clients*, Tom! That is the last time I tell you. If you're part of a team, you must all speak the same language. And yes, seventy is now standard class size for our Mids. It is all in your induction pack. No more questions," she marched out of the room. Tom hurried after her up to the third floor.

Ren was already waiting. As Tom looked at her, she dropped her gaze. He had planned to fix the stupid girl with a dead stare - so wrapped up in her ridiculous fantasies, oblivious to the damage she had caused, desperate for anyone to pay her any attention. She deserved the shame. But now that Tom could face her, after all the time and hurt, he felt only sadness. She looked so small and weak. She had always been a good student. She was just a silly girl.

Without warning, Dickie Vaneman appeared from behind Sophie and whispered into her ear – judging by her stern expression, it was something serious. Tom recognised the man immediately, only he was much shorter than he'd looked on the broadcasts. And fatter. And blotchy, like a marshmallow with lesions.

"Good morning, Sir," said Sophie. "This is Mr. Brown, Mid-level Maths."

Dickie wobbled his chin, "Yes, yes, I know who this is," he squeezed Tom's shoulders and pulled him close. "Just because you forget the people who do all your work for you, don't think I'm so useless. I know *all* of my wonderful staff. I may be in charge of more than a hundred of the greatest damn sites in this Nation, but I know it's the little people that are the glue that makes me look so good," he chuckled, letting go of Tom's shoulders and clasping his arm into a handshake. He clenched Tom's fingers, grinding his knuckles together with a rhythmic crush, peering into his eyes, hoping to see a hint of a wince. He suddenly grasped him by the back of the neck with his free hand and whispered into his ear. "So, Mr. Mid, what's your action plan to make it to the top?"

"I... don't know... I'm only just back," Tom said. "I'm looking forward to remembering how to teach, to be honest!" he laughed at his own joke.

"How ambitious. I'll be sure to remember next time I'm hiring a toilet cleaner." Dickie discarded Tom's hand and grabbed Sophie by the shoulders. "Mrs. Burns, the broadcast team will be here at three. I might be the General of this damn fine institution, but I need my *rock* to join me downstairs?" His voice trailed into a sing-song flirt, "you know how much more beautiful I look when I'm standing next to my beast."

"I'm just building a bridge, sir," she said, giving a cursory nod to the two sullen figures behind her.

"Hurry along," he said. "Get that out of the way. Chop chop," then he placed his thumbs into his belt, rocked on his heels, and vanished as quickly as he'd appeared.

She ushered Ren and Tom into the room.

Sophie finished the meeting after declaring that an emotional bridge had been built. The three of them walked out into the hallway, all making a deliberate effort to avoid eye contact. Tom's sudden tears had created an awkwardness that still hadn't passed. He was disappointed in himself; having concentrated so much on not vomiting, he hadn't considered that he would start weeping.

"Tomorrow is a new day," Sophie said with tired familiarity. "The bridge we have built will allow us to cross the trickiest terrain. Ren, that will be all. Thank you for successfully building. Go home. Arrive on time tomorrow. You still have two unforgiven sins, and if I need to send you to Damascus this term, you will spend the rest of the year as a Low." Ren nodded and began to walk away, flashing a desperate glance at Tom that he ignored. "Tom, spend some time in your room, but you will be off the premises by 11.30 am. You'll need to find me to unlock the main doors to get off-site. Good day." As she turned to walk away, a scream pierced the corridor. A loud, sustained, harrowing shriek.

Ren, who had only reached the middle stairwell doors, froze. Tom and Sophie looked at each other, aware something was truly wrong, the fluttering instinct of catastrophe, like a mother's chill the moment before her child wanders into an oncoming car. Tom walked towards the noise from the west stairwell but quickly recoiled as Dickie burst from around the corner, tripping over his own feet and falling face-first into a display. Scatterings of laminated posters fell on top of him. He heaved himself up and ran towards them.

"RUN!" Dickie panted. "Downstairs... they're mad! THE BASTARDS ARE MAD!"

The lab coat man from the darkroom stumbled from behind the corner where Dickie had appeared. He fell into the same notice board, two dark red stains, one on his right shoulder, the other on his waist, spreading over his white coat. Tom caught him as he collapsed.

"Are you OK?" said Tom, straining under the dead weight slouched in his arms. "Say something..." Tom grasped at the lanyard swinging from the man's neck. He smeared blood from the ID to read the name, "...Zach. Say something."

"They're coming," Zach whispered.

The screaming grew louder. Tom turned to face Dickie and Sophie, huddled outside the Bridge. "Help me!" he said.

"Drag him here now, you imbecile," Dickie hissed. "We need to get downstairs."

The slow shuffle of feet could be heard before the third person appeared around the same corner – a girl. Her every step was deliberate, prowling, but trembling with a tension that removed any grace, like a stray cat relying on one final pounce to avoid starvation.

She stood amongst the scattered posters.

Tom remembered her – Sally Simons, a foul girl who drifted between whichever vile specimen offered her attention. She'd been transferred from another site weeks before his suspension. He had only taught her once, but the experience was soiling. She'd led the class in a sexual moaning chorus, and when Tom had practically begged her to shut up, she instigated a 'kiddy fiddler' chant. Tom had fled the room as she cackled, flicking her tongue between the skinny V of her fingers while all the others drummed their feet. That was the day before Tom had been sent home. Sally was rancid.

She was crying deep, raking sobs. Tom saw a shard of glass gripped so tightly in her hand that it had sunk into the flesh.

"I don't want to do this," she wailed. "I don't want to!" She took a step forward.

"Sally... that's your name, isn't it? Do you remember me?" he kept nodding his head slowly, trying to get her to join in with his rhythm. "I'm Mr. Brown. Sally... calm down, tell me what's wrong."

She stood in front of Tom; Zach still slumped in his arms.

"I don't want to... ... I'm sorry," she said.

"Sally, look at me. What's happened? Just take a breath and tell me. Calm down."

Sally closed her eyes and sniffed, but the tears kept streaming. Her hand moved slowly, but Tom still didn't react as she pushed the end of her shard into Zach's back. He spluttered blood spots onto Tom's face.

Tom yanked Zach to the side, snapping the glass into his back, and shoved his foot into Sally's chest. She staggered backwards and fell to the floor.

"I'm sorry," she coughed, "I didn't want to." She raised her chin to the ceiling and screamed, "UP HERE," then she scrunched her face and bellowed those two words over and over until her voice was just noise.

Tom dragged Zach up the corridor and Sophie ran to help.

"We need an ambulance, now. Ring. *Quickly*!" Tom shouted.

"No!" Dickie ran towards the stairwell in front of Ren. "We need to get out first. This is a no-phone area. We need to get downstairs. Quickly. There are more."

"More what?" Tom's voice was sharp in his ears.

Ren stepped back from the central doors and slowly lifted her arm to point. "They're coming. They're coming up the stairs," she said softly. Dickie peered through the door, then scurried back, dragging the girl with him.

Sally stood up, dug the broken shard from her palm, and walked towards them. "I'm sorry," she said, her voice hoarse from the shouting.

"The Bridge!" Sophie said in a shrill shriek. Tom dropped Zach into her arms and pushed at the door. "The camera, Tom, *always* the camera."

The centre stairwell doors slammed open and a feral stream of teens fell over each other, all filthy with blood and sweat. Shaking their heads like snarled dogs pulling scraps from a bone, they tried to dislodge the Halos tunnelling their vision – a bumbling mass of half-blind rage.

Tom stared at the camera but it blinked red.

"YOU!" Tom pointed at Sophie. "YOU LOOK!"

The mass turned towards them. No individual voice could be heard, just a combined screech.

"WHAT?" her eyes darted between the wild gang at one end of the corridor and Sally at the other.

Tom shoved Sophie towards the door. "I'm only level fucking two," he shouted. "*You* need to open the door."

Sophie gave a panicked breath before nodding her understanding. She stared at the camera. The horde charged, some lowering onto all fours before jumping into the air as they hurtled forwards. The camera blinked green. Dickie barged into the room, bundling Ren with him.

Tom and Sophie dragged Zach in immediately after, planting their feet against the door as a vicious scattering of arms and legs tried to squeeze through. They pushed against the flailing limbs and kicked at the clawing hands, giving one final thrust, slamming the door in its frame.

"That door will be fine," said Sophie. "It's solid. We're fine." The noise continued in the corridor – a chorus of roars and cries for help. Sophie released a deep sigh and stood up, patting down the creases in her tight skirt. "Right. We need to calm down and take back some control here."

Everyone jumped as a bookcase crashed to the floor. Tom stood where he had just toppled it across the door. "I don't care how solid it is. I'm making sure," he said.

Ren started panting and pointing at the floor. "Look! Look! *Look*!" she urged.

Tom bent down and picked up two fingertips – crushed off at the knuckle. He turned and looked through the narrow glass panel in the door and saw one of the pounding hands with splintered bone where two fingers should have been. A face pressed up against the window and blubbed apologies.

Tom faced Sophie and held up the fingers, scraggy and torn at one end but beautifully varnished with a glittering pink, covered in crystal stars.

"What. Is. Going. On?" Tom noticed Dickie shoot a glance at Sophie – a wide-eyed, split-second stare to make sure she kept her mouth shut. "Well?" This time, Sophie and Dickie didn't flinch. Tom knew he wasn't going to get an answer, that he wasn't worthy of knowing whatever it was they weren't saying.

"Tell me. What is going on?" He pocketed the ragged fingertips – as much as they made him feel sick, they seemed too precious to discard. "*What the fuck is going on?*"

3

"THE DAMAGE IS DONE"

The Bridge, with its dark parquet flooring and single-paned, aluminium framed windows, had not only avoided Rego's renovation but still retained many features from its original build. It was a cluttered expanse of board games, odd chairs, and posters with positive quotes driveled under furry faces. Running the length of one wall was a flimsy counter with cupboards – a mini kitchen with sink, kettle, toaster, and plastic plates and cutlery - equipped to feed the needy kids breakfast in a time before too many of the kids became needy.

Sophie grabbed some cushions from the time-out bean bags and placed them on the floor. Tom dragged Zach over and slumped him face-first onto his makeshift bed. He was sweaty and pale, and his face was covered in a bloody grime, his eyes struggling to open under the treacle.

"Zach, I'm removing your coat, OK?" Sophie said as if talking to a foreigner.

Zach gave a slight nod. He winced sharply when loose threads yanked at the embedded glass. Tom helped Sophie roll him onto his side.

"The cut on his stomach isn't deep, more a nasty scratch. He just needs to stop whimpering and man up. It will be fine," said Dickie, pacing the room.

"The shoulder is bleeding a lot, but it looks worse than it is. Maybe if we can cover it up, it will be fine," Sophie pinched Zach's shirt collar and lifted it lightly until the wound couldn't be seen through the tear.

Tom looked at them both and sneered in disbelief, "There's a lump of glass sticking out of a hole in his back. He isn't *fine*, he needs help!"

They rolled Zach onto his front and pulled his shirt up to expose his back. The glass had broken cleanly, its straight edge standing proud of the swollen skin. Zach started shuddering, and with each convulsion, the fresh glisten of blood surged around the thick nub.

Dickie pushed Tom away and clutched the glass with the tips of his fingers. "Fine. Fine. Step aside. At least one of us knows what they're doing."

"What are you *doing*?" Tom said.

"Fixing this mess! Taking charge! Being a man! It will be quick, like removing a plaster."

"No, you fool, leave it in!"

"*Fool*?" Dickie's wide face reddened. "I'm no fool. I am the *C E O*."

"Leave it in, or you'll make it worse," Tom said. "Don't pull it out."

"The damage is done... you utter... you absolute... you... utter... fool."

"Sophie, tell him I'm right," Tom held out his palms, begging for agreement.

"I don't know. Maybe. Karen in reception, or Beryl in finance, they're the first-aiders."

"Karen and Beryl aren't here." Tom sighed. "So, back me up. Tell him we need to leave it in."

Sophie faltered, mouth agape, silenced by the expectation to always defer to Dickie's judgement.

"Only a *fool* would leave it in," Dickie said, still red with rage. "I might've expected Mr. Toilet Cleaner to be a fool. But you surprise me, Mrs. Burns. Are you a fool?"

Sophie shook her head and shrugged.

Zach slowly nodded, "He's right, leave it in."

Dickie huffed and stomped away, planting a portion of his backside on a small plastic chair. The door kept thudding. Ren was crying in the corner. She had tucked her knees up to her neck and hadn't moved.

"Zach, tell us what to do," Tom said.

"My... coat, rip it... press it, hard," his voice kept breaking with a violent shiver.

Tom grabbed the lab coat and quickly tore three long strips.

"I'll put the kettle on," said Sophie. Tom stared at her.

"Great idea, woman," clapped Dickie. "You can make me a brew to clear the air."

"What?" Tom said, staring at him.

"For boiling water, to clean the strips," Sophie said.

"Yes... exactly what I said," Dickie said, "... to clean the strips."

"That's the right thing to do, isn't it, Zach?" Sophie asked, but he didn't respond. The quiver from his lip had spread, his whole body bucked.

"Oh, for goodness sake! I've told you what you need to do. Why do you need to ask him?" Dickie said. "Do as I say, boil some water to clean the strips. Chop chop."

"Fine. Put the kettle on," Tom said. "Dickie come and hold his head. Let him rest on your lap or something."

Dickie walked over to the sink, took the kettle from Sophie, and began filling it up, wafting her away with the back of his hand. She walked over to Zach, struggling against her tight skirt before managing to fold her knees and pull his head up onto her lap.

Zach's waist had stopped bleeding. The slice was covered in a dark crust, so Tom left it. He took a hot, soaked strip from Dickie and tied it tightly around Zach's shoulder, covering the wound.

"How do I tie it around his back?" asked Tom.

Zach suddenly picked himself up onto all fours. Tom grabbed his hips and Sophie held his cheeks as he rocked back and forth, a low gargled moan escaping from his lips.

"What's he doing?" Sophie yelled.

"I don't know," Tom said, "maybe shock. I don't know."

"Ha!" Dickie shouted. "I told you so. He's suffering. Haha! It's because you *fools* left a lump of glass in his back."

Zach slumped again and went quiet.

"We need to hurry. How do I tie it to his back?" Tom repeated.

"Pack them. That's what Zach said. Just squeeze them around it," Sophie said. "What do you think, Dickie?"

"Oh! Now you want to know what I think! Well, I'm afraid this is all on you two medical marvels," he replied. "It has nothing to do with me. At least have the decency to be man enough to take some responsibility."

"Great. Thanks," Tom said, taking two strips from Dickie, squeezing out the excess water, pink from the old blood, and gently draping them either side of the glass. He put his hands on the folded cloth, pressed down hard, and squeezed. The blood and water squelched between the cracks of his fingers. Zach lifted his head, howled, threw up on Sophie's skirt, and passed out. "*He needs an ambulance. We need to call an ambulance. What are we going to do?*"

"Your phone will work on the ground floor. You need to get there," Dickie said.

"What are you saying? We open the door and make a run for it?" Tom pointed at the hands thumping against the smeared glass. "Do we even know how many there are?"

"Twelve. There're twelve of the animals," Dickie said.

"And what do you mean *my* phone? Why would *I* be going?"

"Have some respect, man. Are you suggesting we send a woman?" Dickie walked over and shook Ren by the shoulders, "Or maybe the little girl?" He nudged Zach's backside with his foot, "Or better yet, maybe the bleeding meat sack on the floor," he snorted. "... You absolute fool."

"No. I was thinking you."

Dickie pulled his chin into his neck in disgust, "... I severely damaged my leg when I was helping that young girl escape to safety," he said. "It's a testament to my strength that I managed to save her despite my injury. Not that she has even bothered to thank me yet!"

"Anyway, we'd not get the door shut again, and I wouldn't get more than a few metres. We're trapped."

Dickie walked over to the window overlooking the grass below and pulled at a latch. The window slid forward, letting in a rush of wind.

"Tom! Come and see if you can fit through here! You could climb up to the roof! You could make a call from up there!"

"We're three floors up," Tom said.

"Don't be such a milksop. You have no other choice. I'm embarrassed I didn't think of this sooner. It's obvious. Come and see if you can fit through... chop chop... come and see."

Tom walked over to the window ledge and pressed his face against the glass. Knowing that he wouldn't be able to fit through the gap, he humoured Dickie by lifting himself onto the ledge and squeezing his foot outside. The opening was too narrow for his leg to go further than his knee.

"No chance. We'd need to break the window."

"OK," nodded Dickie. "Let's do that."

"And then what?" Tom barked, finally losing his patience. "Scale the building? I'm not bloody Spiderman! I teach Maths. Look, I'm not climbing out of the window, no way."

"Quit being such a woofter!"

"Shhh! Shut up!" Sophie interrupted.

"Don't you hush me, woman," Dickie said.

"Shut up!" she said. "What is... what is that smell? Is that... apples?"

Tom pulled his leg back from the window gap. Dickie took a deep sniff and wandered slowly to the cupboard.

"In there," Dickie kicked a waist-height tower of building blocks out of the way. "Tom, look in that cupboard... quick, man... *quick*."

Tom dropped from the ledge and opened the cupboard door. Sweet apple-scented smoke wafted into the room. Inside the cupboard, above his head, on the wall opposite the door, was a ventilation grate seeping out a thick white cloud.

He whispered into it, "Hello...? Hello...?"

A sudden thud rattled the grate. Another thud, louder, and a shelf fell off the cupboard wall. A third smash and the plaster below the air vent cracked. The bashing continued and bits of wall flew at Tom. He backed away against the door Dickie had started closing. Tom picked up a long wooden ruler, but quickly dropped it when he saw a plastic baby. He grabbed it by the ankle and held it ready to swing.

There was a crash, and the bottom of a fire extinguisher burst through the cracked plaster. The wall stopped shuddering and the cupboard fell silent, dust floating in the apple air. Then the shiny red extrusion began to creak and squeal as it twisted against the tight hole it had punched through.

Dickie closed the door until there was just a gap he could peek through. Tom tightened his grip on the baby's ankle and positioned himself so that its bulbous skull would smack into anything that poked through. The extinguisher dropped from view with a clang. There was a gaping hole through to an adjoining classroom.

"... Hello?" Tom whispered.

A face popped up. Tom stumbled back and swiped, slamming his baby against a row of books and toppling into the stacked boxes of A4 reams. The boy took a long drag on his Regovape, poked his face through the wall, blew a cloud into the dark cupboard, and smiled. Dickie opened the door, flooding the space with light. The boy looked at Sophie, sitting on the floor, congealing vomit pooled in her lap next to the drooped head of Zach's bloodied body.

"Miss... what the fuck is going on?"

"Language, Dean," Sophie said. "And stop bloody smoking."

4

DEAN SANDLER

Dean listened as his nan pottered outside his bedroom. He turned his back and covered his head with his blanket, knowing what was coming. There was a gentle knock.

"Dean, time to get up, you'll be late," she knocked again. "Dean?"

"Piss off."

Her footsteps disappeared. Dean sat back up in bed and un-paused the arterial spray from the decapitated prostitute's neck, but the bedroom light switched off, followed quickly by the television and the white glow from his console's power button. Dean shifted forward and flicked his wall switch off and on again. Nothing.

His nan shouted from downstairs, "The power'll come back on when you're up. Now get out of bed you little bastard."

He was too late for hot water, and his towel was scrunched into a ball on the floor, so he pulled his tracksuit from under his bed, put it straight on, and walked downstairs.

"I've told all my Bingo ladies that you're on the broadcast tonight," Dean's nan said, not even waiting for him to walk into the room. "This *one* time I ask you to get up, and you're still bloody late," she turned to look at him and started shaking her head violently. "Get back upstairs, now! Get your pigging uniform on."

"No," Dean said flatly. "The letter doesn't say I need it."

"No grandson of mine is goin' on telly to our Nation looking like that. Everyone is watching. You're gonna be famous."

"It's a five-minute segment. The only way it will make me famous is if I whip my cock out... is that what you want, Nan?"

"I'll give you cock," she said; he laughed. "What I want is for you to go and put your uniform on unless you want that games system of yours to be smashed up on the pissing pavement when you get home."

Dean laughed again, "Even you aren't *that* fucking stupid."

"Don't go thinking you've got too big for a whack! Don't test me, I've not got time. I've got a shipment of leaflets, so I'm out delivering all day. I've told everyone about you bein' on tonight. I'm not having you wearing some tatty tracksuit, making *me* look bad. Now go and get changed. There's a pouch in the fridge for breakfast."

Dean had forgotten about his nan's leaflet gig. She'd bid for about ten gigs a week. She was too slow to be a worthwhile Jane, so it was the only way of avoiding scrutiny from the Occupation ministers. Of the ten bids, she'd usually win three or four. A week's work if she went at it flat out, and it made enough to cover their pouches, plus a little leftover for Regovape refills and bingo. But the woman down the road with all the kids had just popped out another, so was undercutting everyone. The leaflet gig was her first that week, and she'd bid a pittance to get it. But it meant she wouldn't be home. Dean got changed without any fuss, knowing he'd just hide for an hour and sneak back when she was out. There was no chance he was going on some shitty broadcast segment.

Dean stepped out onto the pavement and stopped at the neighbour's gate, where he reached his hand through the railing and lifted the latch, letting it swing open. A stocky, little bull terrier bolted out into the street, barking and zig-zagging into the distance, its tongue flapping out of its gaping mouth as though it were smiling. His neighbour came running outside in nothing but a brown towel.

"Bruno!" he yelled. "Bruno!... Dean, you bastard. Bruno! Come back. Bruno!"

The neighbour carried on running, stopping at the top of the road to suck in a few heavy breaths before picking up his solid gut and continuing the chase. Dean knew that if he caught the mutt, he'd belt it to a whimpering wreck, but there was no way that fat prick would catch up. Maybe Bruno would get to enjoy spending a night somewhere without his tail crammed between his quivering legs in a concrete yard filled with shit.

Dean lived on an estate within sniffing distance of the landfill where the nearest village dumped its load. An area where joyride burnouts caused street celebrations. Where the wooden box homes were surrounded by peeling fences collapsed into overgrown lawns and the cardboard-thin walls forced you to listen to every fight, rave, and fuck of every neighbour in the six row rectangles. Every morning he was treated to Mrs. Harvey's toilet symphony – it's how they guessed she'd died – the funny smell, and three straight days without her sploshing gravy wake-up call. And there were seagulls everywhere, huge ones, splattering all below in white, living off the burst bags of rubbish. Dean was under no Nation-induced illusion that it wasn't that bad. But it wasn't the Paradise Flats – a wander through those piss reeking monoliths had taught him it could always get worse.

All the roads in the zones were equal parts tarmac and potholes, dotted with weeds sprouting through the cracks. The street-eyes would only ever light up the nights if they were witnessing a violation. Any memories Dean had outside 102 were as a child. Memories before whole towns became farms, or factories, or were simply abandoned. Before the final schism of Zones and Villages. Before the Joe and Jane initiative occupied the inept to give peace of mind to the Villagers. Memories that had become so faded they merely fuelled sad dreams. The only reason he knew that not everywhere looked broken was because of the glossy pictures underneath the bubble writing in the weekly leaflets.

Dean turned onto the main road as a fleet of grey coaches whizzed by – he recognised a face amongst the depressed cargo – an ex-client who had only left a year ago. They used to be mates, on talking terms at least, he couldn't remember his name. Joes and Janes were the blood in the Nation's arteries, according to the broadcasts – *giving life to the gleaming body* – getting shuttled around in buses the colour of boiled beef. His old mate didn't look happy. They didn't smile at each other. Dean gave up trying to remember his name.

A cup of hot coffee flew towards him and erupted over his chest. A sleek black car from which the drink had been launched, sped over the sprouting grass and broken tarmac into the distance. Dean darted his eyes in search of a brick, but by the time he'd picked up something large enough to throw, the car was gone.

He spat the coffee dripping from his lip, zipped up his coat, ripped a handful of daffodils from a nearby grass patch, and smashed them into bits against a wall. When he had reduced the flowers to frayed stems, he thumped the bricks until the skin on his knuckles lifted, then he turned around to head back home. He didn't care about the argument it would cause. When his nan was pissed off, she was relentless – a tireless, hounding yap. Unending noise with the odd pinch or smack – he'd rather endure that than turn up to site dripping in coffee.

Ren stood in his path. She must have been walking behind him, too embarrassed to say anything. He stifled the genuine smile she evoked, annoyed that things were now so bad between them that she hadn't even said hello.

"Hello," she said.

He looked away.

"I saw what that car did. Are you OK?"

He nodded, shrugged.

"Did it hurt? Is there anything I can do?"

He shook his head.

"Where are you going?" she asked.

"Site. But not anymore. Now home."

"You're supposed to be at site, but you're not going? Won't you get into trouble if you don't turn up? I worry about you."

He rolled his eyes and laughed. Then he budged her aside to carry on walking, but she grabbed his fingers, gently holding his hand in hers.

"Let me sort you out," she said, pulling a pack of tissues from her pocket. She dabbed his face, then unzipped his coat and pressed the tissue flat against his chest until it had soaked through to the shape of her hand. She pulled out another tissue and did the same again. He stared at her the entire time.

"You done?" he said, his face blank, his voice as dismissive as he could manage.

"Yes," she pulled away. "Please go to site, don't go home."

"What's it to you?"

"Don't be like that."

"Fuck off!" he said and kept walking.

"Well at least walk me through the alley," she said. He stopped. "Otherwise, I'll be late. I've got to be on-site as well. I can't walk through the alley alone."

Dean laughed. The only reason she'd say she needed to be at site, he thought, was because she wanted him to ask her why. As if he cared. He refused to look at her as he turned back to walk her through the shortcut. She followed a few strides behind.

When they got to the fence after the alley, Ren took one look inside reception and stopped walking. Dean carried on, with the coffee dry and his temper calmed, he decided he might as well go in. He left Ren loitering, kicking her feet against the gravel and staring at the pavement.

There were eleven others waiting in reception. Dean knew eight of them, seven from site and one from reputation – a lad called Bradley Sherrington. The other three he hadn't seen before, but they had the scarred scowls that meant they didn't seem out of place.

Dean sat on the corner of the reception table, on the fringes of the group, watching as they sized each other up. Casey Richardson was trying to pretend he hadn't seen Dean swagger in. He was forcing a laugh to prove he wasn't shitting himself, constantly flicking his floppy, lop-sided fringe to one side.

"Alright, Casey, mate?" Dean shouted. "I ain't seen you for a while. You wanna come over and give me a cuddle?" Casey fixed his ferret eyes on the floor. "Sally, you filthy bastard! No kiss?" he patted the empty space next to him.

Sally Simon skipped over and sat down. Dean had spent the last couple of weeks trying to talk her into giving him a blowie. All the signs were there, he thought, he'd put in enough effort and the girl never stopped giggling when she was with him, but he'd not yet managed to get the tease to stick her head down.

"Do you like my nails? My mum did 'em," she held up a set of pink, sparkling tips.

Dean took her hand and looked for long enough that he could stroke her arm a few times, then he placed it on his lap, high up enough to make her smile.

"Yeh. Nice," he finally said. "I'd like 'em more scratching down my back."

"Shut up!" she replied, snorting with laughter.

She took her hand off his lap and scraped her fingertips over his shaved head. When she stopped, Dean nudged her to continue, so she did.

Without warning, Bradley Sherrington shouted, "How long are we gonna be fucking waiting?"

He booted the reception stand and leaflets scattered into the air, littering the floor. One of them flapped into the face of a newbie, who batted the paper away and tutted but quickly smiled. A second newbie kicked a stray leaflet in agreement. But the third sneered as a glossy page skimmed the back of his head, a tiny mutter, the words 'dick head.' Quiet, but it was enough. Brad was quick. Before anyone could decide whether to pick sides and join in, his thick fingers were squeezing the newbie's throat. Brad pushed him back against the door and crunched their foreheads together, pinning the back of his head against the glass.

"Whatthefuckyoufuckingprickfucking..." the newbie said as Brad scrunched his face between the thumb and fingers of his rough hands, a tip of his nose poking out from the squeezed folds of the face. Brad opened his jaw and clamped the boy's bony bridge in his mouth. "Owowowow-fuckownoFUCKnofuckFUCK...." he begged.

Brad bit down hard for a brief second, then slowly pulled his teeth away, still close enough to latch back on in an instant. Dean could see the crescent indent on the newbie's nose left by Brad's teeth.

"You disrespect me again, and I will eat your fucking face. Understand?" The newbie nodded quickly. "Now, say thank you."

"What?"

Brad slid his thumbs up the boy's squashed face and pushed them into his eyes.

"Nofuckowfuckno…thankyouthankyouFUCKTHANK YOU."

Brad released him and stood in the centre of the reception, his head panning slowly from side to side, surveying the response. The corridors had been whispering about Brad for a while – some new client, huge and fucking horrible, relocated to 102 for failing his classification year for the third time. Dean had thought it couldn't be true – no-one got that many chances before delabelling, plus it would make him at least nineteen. He stared at Brad; Dark, tight curls sitting on shaved back and sides, towering over everyone. But it wasn't just his size and stubble (although he did look old). His presence was stifling. It had a gravity, like the heavy air around him would swallow you if you didn't keep clear. He *was* different. A bear in a dog pit, shaped by struggle. The other kids were practically drooling as they admired from the corner of their eyes. Brad caught Dean's gaze and stared back, instantly lowering his forehead and tensing. Dean smiled and looked away – there was no need to test this thick bull. Not yet.

Mrs. Burns marched through the main entrance and raised an eyebrow at the mess.

"This way, please, Subs," she said. The response was too slow for her liking. "Move, now!" she snapped. "If you want to take home your free Block today, you *will* follow my instructions *immediately*. Now get your Halos on and get into the B-suite, or go home. Make your choice, but do *not* waste my time."

Dean smirked as all of them, including Brad, lined up quietly at the Halo gate. Forget reputations, you offer something shiny, and any animal will beg. She shepherded the clients under the metal arch, holding her Block against the rubber strap around their heads after they'd pulled the goggles down. They walked away to the B-suite as the archway shot out another hanging Halo for the next Sub. Mrs. Burns looked at Dean when there was no one else left. He hadn't strayed from his table edge – no matter what they have, if you force yourself to want nothing, you're not theirs.

"Dean, come into the hall, now," she ordered.

"Nope."

"Or you won't get your Block."

"So?"

"Dean! Now!"

"I don't give a fuck. Send me home," he slumped forward, staring outside.

"Dean, I cannot keep giving you chances-"

"Good," he said. "Don't. Send me home. Kick me out."

"This is it, Dean, your last chance. Do you know where you go if you drop out of Subs?"

"I don't fucking care."

"Stop trying to be tough," she said. "I see through it."

"I'm not *trying*, *Sophie*," he sighed. "I *don't* care."

"Dean!"

"Fuck off!"

"*Dean!*"

"Fuck off, slag!"

"..."

The insult stuck in the air, brewing in the quiet. Sophie's stony glare broke, a sight rarely witnessed, and only ever by Dean. Her eyes glistened, "Please, Dean. Please," she begged. "You need to sit through one presentation with me, a quick talk with someone else, learn what to say, and the broadcast crew will be in and out before you know it. *Please.*"

"You're crying?... Are you fucking kidding? You're fucking crying... ..." he pointed at her, teary, but refusing to blink. "This is an ugly fucking look for you." He stood up and walked under the arch, snatching a headset from its hook.

Mrs. Burns wiped at her cheeks, took a sharp breath, swept her hands down her suit jacket, and followed. Dean pulled the goggles over his eyes and she held her Block against them. There was a soft whir as the strap pinched around the back of his head and the seal around his eyes sucked to his face. They walked into the B-suite together.

It was a large, double-height hall with thick black curtains hanging around the perimeter. Automated tiered seating rolled out in layers from the back, creating a 300-seat auditorium. If you stood on the back row, next to the exit onto the first-floor corridor, you could almost reach the ceiling. When the seats were rolled out, it created two narrow passageways either side of the hall and a small stage area at the front, just proud of the touchwall – a monumental screen to deliver its message to the ignorant.

They walked through a gap in the curtains surrounding the hall. The seating was out. But the other Subs were nowhere to be seen, just faint chuckles and shushing.

"COME OUT THIS INSTANT!" Mrs. Burns' voice was a rasping scream. "You all have exactly ten seconds to get out from under there and find a seat. Ten. Nine..." feet scrabbled and voices muttered in panicked hilarity as Subs toppled out either side from under the seating. "If I ever see any of you under there again... You could be killed!" she was still screaming. "Seats! Sit down! Now! Now! Now!" the Subs ran up the aisle to the back row as Mrs. Burns' voice started to crack. "*The front row!* NOW!" the neck veins below her crimsoned scowl throbbed. The giggling continued as they all trudged down to the first row. Dean slumped in a chair on the front right corner. Mrs. Burns closed her eyes and took one long, slow, deliberate breath to pull herself back from the brink. "... Ready for Halos!" she said, anger still coursing through her words. Dean's clear lenses turned opaque and everything went dark.

After the presentation, Mrs. Burns lined the Subs up. They watched with childish awe as she pressed the red button on the wall and the tiered seating clunked back until all twelve rows had folded into the wall. Mrs. Burns darkened their Halos so they had to be frog-marched, hand in hand, to A-suite. She gave them back their sight when she ordered them in.

A man in a lab coat was standing nervously in front of the touchwall. Block in one hand, and scribbled notes on the inside of his other. It was obvious to Dean that this guy was clueless. His stupid mouth flitted between a soft perma-grin and a tight purse. The constant twitching made his flimsy goatee bob up and down; it was like staring into a cat's irritated arsehole. And he wouldn't stop blinking. He looked weak. Dean just needed Mrs. Burns to leave, then he would walk straight out.

"Good morning, greetings, salutations, *mane bonum*, one and all. I am Zachary Nob…" Mrs. Burns shook her head disapprovingly. He started again. "I am *Mr.* Noblie-Goggins," he stared at her until she nodded at him to continue. "I'm sure you are all super excited," he waited for a response, but there wasn't one. "… Well just stay calm. Dr. Vaneman, who is a cool fellow, is coming in today. To see *you*. Imagine that, the CEO, taking time out to meet *Subs*."

Dean dropped his head against his desk, distracting Noblie-Goggins with the clunk. Brad started laughing, so the other Subs laughed too.

Mrs. Burns stepped away from the wall where she had been leaning, "The next one of you that makes a noise will be sent home. Immediately. I repeat. You do not have to be here today. Is that clear? Try and behave like normal human beings for the next few hours, not like a bunch of… Subs. Understand?"

"No," shouted Dean.

"Outside now!" she snapped. Dean let out a howl and skipped out of the room. Mrs. Burns hissed a final warning at the remaining Subs before joining him in the corridor. "I'm *not* sending you home. *Do you understand?* I am *not* sending you home. Now, I have a meeting I need to attend. Please, please, go back into the room and just behave. You are not going home."

"… He's called Noblie-Goggins… *Noblie… Goggins…* I mean, I'm definitely taking the piss out of that. I've too much fucking respect for myself *not* to take the piss… Noblie-fuck-ing-Goggins," Dean laughed.

"You will behave. You *will*. You are not going home."

"Fuck off."

"…There's so little left that your mother would be proud of," Sophie said.

Dean paused, burning with hate. He stared at her and wanted to spit. He hated her business suits and expensive shoes, her hard face, and her ugly, short hair. He hated the way she spoke to him so different from the way she spoke to anyone else. He hated her so much, that it took all his effort to pretend he didn't care.

Raucous laughter broke out in the classroom. Mrs. Burns flashed a stern eye at the camera and shoved the door open the moment it clicked. She stuck her head in the room and delivered a fresh bout of fury. Dean glanced at the Block poking out from her pocket. He hovered his fingers, then plucked it out and pocketed it with the speedy silence of a practised thief, instantly dropping any expression of guilt.

She slammed the door and turned to Dean, who had already prepared his look of innocent regret.

"Fine, *Sophie*, fine," he said, holding up his hands. "Sorry. I'll behave. I promise."

She held a long, suspicious silence, then nodded and walked back towards the main entrance.

Dean smiled. He held the stolen Block against his Halo and pulled it from his head when the strap relaxed. He stared into the camera box and kicked the door open. Mr. Noblie-Goggins jumped.

"Pardon me, Nob Gog, please, fucking continue," Dean said as he strutted in.

Noblie-Goggins laughed nervously and opened his mouth to carry on, but Dean drowned out his voice with a deep belch. The seated Subs started to giggle and fidget, anxious to involve themselves.

"Mrs. Burns has sent me home," Dean shouted. "So, I'm going!"

"Yes, fine, sure," he replied, nodding vigorously. "If that is what she has done, absolutely, good, go home. Please."

"Later, Bitches," Dean said. The Subs started whooping as Dean sauntered to his seat and picked up his coat. "You coming, Sally? I've got an idea for something I can do with that mouth of yours."

She reddened, "I can't," she whispered. "I want my Block."

"Fucking tease," he smiled. "Suit yourself."

As Dean walked out, he barked in Mr. Noblie-Goggins' face, who stumbled back against the touchwall. He waited for the weakling to start talking again before slamming the door as he left, to disturb him one final time.

Dean stood quietly in the corridor. He could hear Mrs. Burns' nasal nag, so he pushed through the centre stairwell doors and ducked against the wall. Her voice disappeared down the corridor. His nan would still be in the house, and he didn't fancy wandering the streets for an hour, so he decided to find a room to hide in. After sitting on the cold concrete steps until it became uncomfortable, he picked himself up and vaulted up the stairs to the top floor. A sign read:

'This floor is for high-level staff and Tops only – anyone else entering without permission is guilty of a grave sin.'

Dean spat on the sign and opened the double doors. He stopped outside the Bridge when he heard voices, ducking under the window in the door and placing his ear against the wall. He gave an obligatory chuckle to the sound of sobbing, and continued down the corridor, turning the corner to stand outside the classroom opposite the West stairwell. He pulled out his stolen Block to unlock the Top-access door and let himself in.

Dean had managed to scrawl cock pictures on half the desktops before being jolted by an echoing scream. He walked back out of the classroom, through the double doors at the top of the stairwell, and peered over the balcony. The screaming continued. He saw the top of a big, bald head bounding up the stairs. The bald man glanced at Dean as he stumbled halfway up the final flight, wide-eyed and panting. The sweaty mass shoved his arms out in front of him and held up his hands as a shield.

"You... You're one. Aren't you?"

Before Dean could answer, the man slapped him hard across the face. Dean fell back against the banister as the man shoved past and disappeared onto the top corridor.

"I CAN'T STOP... SORRY!" a voice screamed from the ground floor, unrestrained and vicious, like a snared animal.

Dean peeked over the balcony again. He saw Noblie-Goggins stumbling up the stairs, covered in blood. Dean didn't hesitate; he ran back through to the corridor and darted into his classroom.

Behind the walls and slammed door, the muffled chaos got louder. It had to be terrorists, thought Dean, anti-nationalists running around the building. The leaflets were always warning about them. He yanked a fire extinguisher from its plastic housing and had a swift practice of caving in an extremist's head, then he hid under a desk.

After ten minutes of growing used to the distant banging, Dean loaded up his Regovape and flicked it on.

5

"YOU ARE NOT TAKING ME WITH YOU"

Dickie and Tom pulled Dean through the extinguisher hole. When he had brushed off the dusting of plaster, he repeated himself.

"What's going on? It's terrorists, isn't it?"

"No," said Dickie. "It's those blinking, filthy Subs. I knew this was a bad idea. This facility is supposed to be a business, not some flaming charity for mongrels."

"*I'm* a Sub," Dean did a double-take as he recognised Dickie. "You're the fat prick that slapped me. You fat prick."

"Ahh, yes, about that," Dickie held up a hand and flopped it around as if trying to swat away the accusation, "we... fell, it was... an accident. I didn't hit you. If anything, you hurt my arm when you stumbled into me."

"You hit him?!" Sophie balked. "*When?*"

"*No.*" Dickie insisted. "Let me be absolutely clear and state on record, I did not hit him. Trust me, he'd know about it if I had. I repeat, accidental, no harm caused."

"Whatever, prick," Dean said.

Dickie clenched his floppy hand into a fist, "I suggest you don't swear at me again, laddo."

"What do you mean, it's the Subs?" Dean said, then he whispered, just loud enough for all to hear, "…prick."

"We all saw the animals, ransacking the corridors – they're sick! They've assaulted Zach. He needs a doctor, urgently, God protect him. Now they've trapped us in here, in this room. Barbarians. They're sick."

"It's more than that," Sophie said. "As wild as you think these things might be, this is not normal… even for Subs."

"Mrs. Burns. Be very careful. Instead of gossiping like some ditz, let's just consider the facts." Dickie pointed at his clammy fingers as he listed each point, "We have crazy Subs running riot. Zach needs medical care. And the only way we can get help is either there," he pointed at the door, "or out there," he pointed at the window.

A fresh round of thudding shook the door. Ren's quiet sobbing continued. Dean noticed her, and a spike of warmth spread a stupid grin across his face. He couldn't help it; when he didn't have time to consider his response, he still liked seeing her. The best thing about being held back a year was that he got to share some classes with her. There was something about the way she spoke, and listened, and laughed. She could be so cutting, but never in a way that hurt, and so warm, without being sentimental. Dean was rarely honest with anyone, but during a few lessons, she had managed to lull out unguarded sentences with just a look. Ren didn't know it, but for a while, it was their time together that helped him gain back balance, gifting him small moments of feeling something again. Then she became obsessed with Mr. Brown, and turned into someone else, leaving him ashamed that he was ever soft enough to be disarmed.

"Ren, what you doing here?" As if the cogs quickly whirred in his head, he pointed at Tom and gasped, mouth open in mock shock. "Of course! You're here for him! Ren and Browny, together again. How you doin', Mr. Shagsy? Good to see you again. I heard you'd gone mental."

"No, Dean!" Ren choked through her tears. "Stop it. It was a stupid lie. I made it up. Just shut up!"

Her upset caused him a tinge of embarrassment, but he persisted.

"… Course you made it up, even the Specials knew that," he pointed at Tom again. "You seen him? Nowt says adult virgin more than limp dick, shitty shoes over there. I've heard you only go for real men. You like it rough."

"Dean!" Sophie said. "For one single second, stop being the most unpleasant version of yourself. Please!"

"You're so awful," Ren said softly.

Dean wanted to apologise to her, he was desperate for them to be alone so he could, but they had an audience, so he laughed instead.

*   *   *

Tom regarded the boy, Dean, frustrated that he felt compelled to respond. Frustrated that a *boy* was insulting him. "Actually, I have a wife." Frustrated because the boy was right. "...Had ... had a wife." He stared at Ren as the room went quiet. She went back to sobbing. Tom snapped. He picked up a stool, walked over to the window, and slammed the metal feet against the glass – he was so fed up with being the loser. He raised the stool back above his head and clattered it again – the boy was right to call him a limp dick. He cracked the window into a web of tiny squares with a swing that felt like it tore his shoulders – from now on he was going to be the man he needed to be. The final smash made the glass explode, the cubes flying out onto the playing fields below, a rush of cool air blew through his hair – no more nights crying on the sofa amongst the stiff tissues and biscuit crumbs. "OK. I'm going out the window. Someone has to save us," he said, picking himself back up onto the ledge and standing by the empty frame. The wind howled and rippled against his clothes. He scraped the bottom of his foot against the remaining cubes stuck in the rubber seal. He clasped his right hand around the window handle so tightly his knuckles whitened as he leaned his entire body out into the open air – it was time to be the man his absent wife deserved. He looked down at the grass. It was an awfully long drop, Tom thought, so he jumped back onto the floor and sat down. "Not a chance. Not a bloody chance."

"Fuck me! Shitty shoes. It's no wonder your wife ran off with Black Barry!" Dean said, laughing. "Out my way, limp dick." He pulled himself up onto the window ledge but

Sophie immediately grabbed him by the back of his trousers and pulled him down.

"Absolutely not. No way," she said. "You're staying right here. I'm not having *you* plunge to your death."

"Oh... thanks," said Tom.

"That's not what I meant," Sophie snapped. "Dean is a child."

"Don't be soft," Dean said. "I'd rather be up on the roof than stuck in this room with you cock lickers. I'll be up in two minutes, call the Crusaders, sorted."

"I agree with Mrs. Burns. The boy stays," added Dickie, hurriedly. He walked over to the empty frame and looked down. "Mr. Brown, pull yourself together, come on, man."

"You do it!" said Tom.

"Stand up, man," Dickie said. "The roof can't be more than a few metres above the window. If it weren't for my leg, I'd be up there in a shot. When I was your age, I was still climbing scaffolding so I could build a company from nothing. This is the problem nowadays; people aren't prepared to do what's necessary. I've done my climbing. I reached the summit. C E O. There is nothing above me now. I'm not some cog. Whereas you, Mr. Brown-"

"Have shit shoes," Dean said.

Dickie ignored him, "You're the right man for this job. Stop giving me excuses for why you're going to fail and succeed. It's pathetic."

Tom looked around the room. Zach's chest was still slowly lifting with each long breath. His face looked calm, resting in Sophie's sick-crusted lap, but there was no way of knowing how bad he was. He needed help. Tom climbed back up onto the window frame. This time he kept his eyes pointing at the sky as he leaned out.

"There's a pipe," Tom shouted. "Above the window. If I had something long, I could reach it," he jumped back down and darted his eyes around the room. "Your belt," he said to Dickie. "Give me your belt."

Dickie frowned, "Be bloody careful. That's imported sea turtle," he said as he slipped it off.

Tom removed his belt and threaded it through Dickie's buckle, he pulled until both buckles met and gave a second tug to test its strength. Tom moved with determined vigour as he jumped back up to the frame.

"My legs, you two, hold my legs, quick," Tom said.

Dickie grabbed the top of Tom's left leg.

"Piss off, pervert. I ain't grabbing your leg," Dean said. "It's too close to your bollocks. Who'd you think I am? Ren?"

"Shut up!" Ren said, poking her head up to shout before retreating into her arms.

"Yes, Dean, do us all a favour and shut up. Now go and grab Mr. Brown's legs." Sophie said.

Dean slowly stood up and wrapped his arms around Tom's right thigh, "You best have tucked little limp dick to the other side."

Facing into the room, Tom shuffled his feet until his heels were over the window's edge, then he slowly leaned backwards. His stomach strained and his jeans started to slide under the desperate grasps holding him in.

"Do not let go!" he shouted.

"You bloody well make sure you don't fall. If you do, you are not taking me with you!" Dickie shouted back.

Dean gave a jerking nod and went back to squeezing. Tom held the makeshift rope in his right hand and looked up. Poking out of the building's smooth facia and pointing all the way up to the roof, a metre above the window, was a thick black pipe. If Tom could get to the pipe, he was confident he could climb to the top. He flapped his long belt, missing it completely. It took four swipes until it looped over the pipe's bend.

"The ruler!" shouted Tom. "Ren, get me the ruler, from the cupboard."

Still crying, she quickly held up the wooden stick. Tom relaxed the grip of his left hand on the window handle and let go. A prickling pulse shot through his arms and a fresh slip of sweat chilled his palms as he leaned further out into the cold. He snatched the ruler from Ren and held it above his head, prodding the end of the belt with it, then, with a flick, teased it further over the pipe's bend. He repeated the motion until it was hanging within reach. The acid burned his shaking thighs with every slight move.

"OK. On three," Tom said.

He flung the ruler back into the room and snatched the end of the belt with his free hand. On his tiptoes, leaning out of a four-storey high window, both thighs embraced, with his arms at full stretch clinging on to two belts looped around a thick plastic pipe – Tom suddenly questioned the wisdom of his plan. His knees started trembling. A mixture of sheer terror, and the knee knocking into his face, made

Dean start laughing – his rote response to any situation. Dickie was hugging so tightly that he had pulled Tom's jeans below the buttons on his boxer shorts. Tom gripped his belt ends and waited for his knees to calm. Eventually, all went silent.

"OK," Tom shouted. "I can do this. Get ready... one, tw-"

"Don't phone the Crusaders!" Dickie bellowed.

"What?"

"The authorities. Don't phone them. When you get on the roof, phone the Rego switchboard, and ask for Mr. Drexler. Don't phone the Crusaders."

"What?!" Tom snarled. He pulled his eyes away from the pipe and glanced at Dickie.

A belt buckle snapped. Tom fell away from the window. As he flew backwards his entire body stung with panic. His arms frantically swam through thin air, and the desperate tug of hands buried into his legs. His vision span through the clouds to the ground below and his scream echoed over the field. Tom's back thumped against the wall and he coughed misty breaths. The world was upside down. The screams from above slowly replaced the howling in his ears.

"Tom! Tom! Are you OK?"

"Up!" he screamed. "Pull me up now."

The inside of Tom's knees creaked with the strain of Dickie and Dean pinning them against the frame. They felt ready to pop. Stray glass cubes scraped into soft flesh but the pain barely registered. Sophie flopped Zach's head onto the cushion and clambered up onto the window frame. She straddled Tom's legs and slowly reached her arm out of the window. Dickie and Dean yanked, pulling Tom over the frame up to his bottom. His jeans were now by his ankles and his groin was squashed up against Sophie's face as he grasped her outstretched hand. Dean succumbed to another bout of manic laughter and Sophie kept yelling at him to 'shut up,' her voice muffled by Tom's testicles. With one final huge pull, everyone fell back into the room.

Tom trembled as he pulled his jeans back up, Sophie wiped his sweat off her chin, Dickie remained on all fours, panting. Their heads all angled to avoid any accidental stares, like the shameful silence shared by strangers during a hungover morning in a cheap hotel. Sophie crawled back to Zach, who had started to stir in the commotion, and continued nursing him.

"Send Dean up," Dickie finally mumbled. "As the boy said, he's a fit young lad. And he willingly volunteered. It's his choice, his responsibility."

"He is *not* going up," Sophie's tone was soft enough not to startle Zach but stern enough that Dean didn't bother trying to argue.

"... Why shouldn't I call the Crusaders?" Tom said, sitting up. "Why did you tell me not to ring them?"

"Because the broadcasters will be here in a matter of hours. We don't need a bumbling bunch of incompetents adding to the rigmarole."

"Rigmarole?" Tom gestured at the blood-soaked rags and nub of glass sticking out of Zach. He pointed at the shattered window frame. He nodded towards the classroom door, still being pounded intermittently, a macabre metronome, scratching at what little patience remained. "I think we are a little bit past rigmarole."

"Do you know how many clients... parents... how many *teachers* rely on me?" Dickie said. "Not just this site, but all my sites across the Nation? Let me teach you a thing or two about leadership. Listen up, Sophie, Lord knows you could do with a reminder. Do you think a great leader would put his people in jeopardy? I won't let this be twisted into some fake scandal. A great leader protects. He doesn't admit to mistakes because he doesn't make them."

"Bollocks!" Tom ran the tip of his tongue over his top lip as he decided whether to let his temper take over. "You're lying. I know your sort. Expecting everyone to worship you if you let us lick the grease from your fingers. Do you hold your nose when you drive into a zone? Pray for your car? Have you seen the streets around this site? People round here have nothing to be grateful for. Nothing you've ever done has been good for them. YOU are everything wrong with this Nation."

"Retract that, immediately!" Dickie's cheeks suddenly inflated with a coughing burst that made his eyes stream. "You owe me an apology. As your CEO, I demand it. I have starred in fourteen broadcasts, I'll have you know. Fourteen! I've been on the cover of the Nation's leaflets more times than you've had hot meal pouches. I've been nominated for a Minister's Pride Award, for heaven's sake!"

"They eat pouches cold, you pus sack," Tom said. "And we all know what's required to join the Pride list."

"What are you implying?" Dickie said, his eyes narrowing.

"That you swallowed a line of dicks for a trophy," Dean interrupted.

Sophie pointed at Dean with such rigid anger her finger looked like it would snap backwards. Dean laughed and used his tongue to keep prodding out his cheek, letting frothed spit drip down his chin as he choked on imaginary ejaculate.

"RETRACTION!" Dickie shouted. "I demand a retraction. How dare you question the sanctity of our great Nation and its ministers. How dare *you* question *me!* I've a mind to report you for immoral values."

"DO IT!" Tom said. "I've got lots to tell them."

"… *This…* …this is merely a problem that needs to be solved… nothing more." Dickie gently lowered a hand, appealing for calm. "I've been doing it all my life. It's what I do. I don't make excuses. I get the job done. So, we have a few Sub animals behaving like Sub animals. What are we going to do? Cry like little girls, or solve a problem?"

"*Shut up!*" Tom stepped forward, nose to nose with Dickie, refusing to let things mellow. "You're a bully! A cheat! Standing on the shoulders of all the miserable bastards you've fisted on your climb."

"Spare me the foul-mouthed waffle, Mr. Brown. Let's have some civility, thank you. I have been a saviour to more lives than you could ever hope to imagine. Clients, thousands of them, all with positive destinations, because of me. Clients in Rego sites *never* fail, because of me."

"*Well, you're not fucking teaching them anything then!*" Tom peppered Dickie's red face with flecks of spit.

"Stop it!" shouted Sophie. "Stop it.... just *stop*. This is stupid. We're not getting on the roof, so calling the Crusaders, *or* Mr. Drexler, is out of the question. We need to think of something else."

"*Like what?*" Tom swivelled.

"...I don't know."

"You mean out there, through *them?*" He pointed at the door.

"*I don't know.*"

Zach slowly raised his head, "We need to turn them off." All eyes, apart from Dickie's, turned to look at him, even Ren stopped sobbing. "My Block is downstairs, in the A-suite. If we can get that, we can turn them off."

6

SOPHIE BURNS

Sophie was awake to cancel her alarm before it woke her husband. She hadn't slept properly since becoming the GM – she only set the thing out of habit. She crept out from under her covers and into the bathroom. The door creak was quiet, but she still darted a glance back to see whether Jamie had stirred.

She pointed her face up into the shower and let the hot water stream over her. She'd stand there for hours if she could, covered in noise and warmth. It was the only place where thoughts didn't trouble her. But the shower always had to end, and everything returned with the dripping cold.

She sneaked back into the bedroom. Jamie's back was still turned, but Sophie could see that his boxer shorts were now at the foot of the bed. She didn't have the energy for his sulking, so, as per the routine, she removed her towel and climbed back under the covers. He spun around eagerly and rolled on top, pushing himself in uncomfortably quickly. Sophie turned her head away from his grunting, managing to find some small pleasure in the thought of having to shower again.

Sophie waited at the kitchen door to let Jamie through first – that way they wouldn't need to squeeze in together. Whatever they used to have had politely died long ago. She couldn't remember what his eyes looked like. She had planned to get to work early, but, thanks to him, would now need to stay late. Knowing that she'd have to sacrifice her evening jog, she only placed a single slice of granary in the toaster.

"I won't be back until late. I have a meeting that will run on," he said.

Sophie greeted his lie with relief, "OK," she smiled.

"And please remember to contact the agency. Imagine how much more time we'd have together if we had our own Janet to do all your little jobs."

"Enjoy your day," she said.

He left. She had no intention of contacting the agency. And not just because anyone they got would probably be an ex-client, but because she didn't want some sad girl ghosting around *her* house. Plus, the neighbours already gawked at her fresh food and posh clothes – imagine the torrent of violent whispers if they got their own Janet! One more bag of excrement through the letterbox and Jamie would start to win the argument about moving to a village where "their type belonged." Sophie wasn't ready to turn her back on who she was. Not for him.

She placed her Block on the granite counter and flicked through the Nation's news, turning off the screen when it became too depressing. She stared at the crisp, cold lines of her kitchen, the surfaces landscaped with gleaming gadgets, four tattered screw holes where the flimsy wall couldn't take the weight of the reclaimed oak floating shelf. Jamie had arranged for the entire refit as a surprise. She sliced a second piece of bread and placed it in the toaster. She hated her kitchen.

A gaggle of neighbours was standing by her fence, one leaning against it. They silenced when she stepped outside, heightening the babble from her marble fountain. The entrance up to her home was a gaudy, flowering, pristine barrier to the estate around it (another renovation secretly initiated by Jamie) — a loud statement isolating them from their inferior surroundings. She hated her front garden.

The neighbours didn't part ways when Sophie opened her gate. She had to traverse their contempt. Someone had spat on her car door handle, a thick wadge, but Sophie noticed it in time.

Since the 'Nation's Birth,' hatred defined its initial years. Ignorance had been distilled by fear, and the resentment had been stoked until it was a fog trapped inside the new borders. Discourse was drowned out, insults were screamed over reason, and the dense were manipulated into embracing the worst qualities of the greediest people. Nothing got better. The newfound sovereignty solved *nothing,* and nationwide rage finally erupted like a lanced boil. The Corporate Conflict was brutally swift, people's swollen fury immediately giving way to exhaustion. The Ministers and Rego were accepted as long as everyone was allowed to quietly clench on to their puffed rage. The pockets of poverty spread and the wealthy little bubbles of glamour locked themselves away in shrinking villages. Jamie was desperate to move to one. Whenever Sophie had accepted invitations to exclusive evenings and ventured out from the vitriol of her zone, she understood the lure. But she couldn't ignore the relentless Champagne chatter – the self-interested, self-justifying, self-aggrandising absurdity from the alarmingly shallow and abundantly stupid. Politely stifling her disgust behind clenched teeth and rolled eyes because the food was good, the alcohol sparkling, and at least the falsehoods were masked with pleasantries.

She looked again at the spit on her door handle. Maybe she didn't belong. As much as posh parties made her want to jab olive sticks into her eyes, life would be easier. She pinched the edge of the handle to open the door and the gaggle behind her began sniggering. These people weren't who she was, and her hatred of her husband didn't mean he wasn't right. This was no place to raise a family.

Sophie arrived at site and pulled into her parking space, she looked at the clients loitering in reception and watched as one of the new ones slammed his foot into the leaflet stand.

"Bradley Sherrington... profile," she said to her Block.

"Bradley Sherrington. Classification year, fourth attempt. Client label, Sub. Demoted from Special after grave sin, assault on a teacher," the Block responded.

She repeated the description. She memorised *all* client profiles – one of so many habits to convince herself that she might make a difference.

"Behaviour strategies," she said.

"Guardian co-operation, ineffective. Non-verbal challenge, ineffective. Public challenge, detrimental. Recommendations, repeat simple instruction script. Additional information, client has been placed on CTRL programme," her Block replied.

Sophie walked into the building and ignored the mess. She had to start quickly. Subs would fill any silence with chaos, and it was immediately obvious that Dean was going to be even more difficult than usual. There was no way she could send him home. She was so tired of defending him, but she had no choice – no matter how *awful* he was. But this was his last chance.

When she had finally settled the Subs on the front row in the B-suite, she didn't even have the energy to read her presentation, so she played her recording through their Halos. Their eyes disappeared behind black as the touchwall flickered into life. Sophie's face filled the screen. She grasped respite during the rare moments at work when she could break character. It was vital that she maintained her grip, recently it was becoming near impossible to cover every crack. Sophie slumped her shoulders, relaxed her face, rubbed the discomfort in her stomach, and tried to ignore the sound of her voice through the speakers.

"Congratulations, once again, for being the lucky nominees to take part in Rego's latest innovation. As the first clients in our Nation to receive this revolutionary aid, you will be the brave pioneers that make history. As a thank you for making the right choice to become CTRL clients, you will receive your very own Block," some of the Subs started whooping.

"As an inclusive site, every client matters. But, if you graduate from a zone site, the only way you can avoid a named occupation, is if you are a Top, and even then, it is rare. And you are all *Subs*. If you avoid delabelling, you might escape a future on the Lines, maybe you'll be a Jane or Joe if you're lucky.

"With CTRL, we guarantee that you will not fail. With CTRL we guarantee that, even though the choices you have made have led you here, those choices no longer need define you. With CTRL we guarantee you can become something more than you are... you can become something better," she stifled a cringe at her recorded recital of the company message.

The screens then played The Woodland Parable – showing the animated propaganda was a Rego ritual, like prayers before sodomy. No expense had been spared in its creation, even drafting in a famous director. It was policy that every student watched the short film at least once a term. Sophie had seen it too many times. Her fixed smile and flushed shame, a Pavlovian response to the opening chimes that accompanied a tentative rabbit straying from its warren.

During the slow ten minutes, a selection of forest creatures, with the misguided notion that they should venture from their habitats, are almost devoured by the greedy fox.

Only when Roland, Ribbit, Floppy, and Hoot return to their kind, are they able to finally understand the safety in accepting who they are.

The cartoon built to its inspirational crescendo, with the creatures disbanding and tearfully embracing their kin as the fox prowls off into the moonlight in search of some other delusional rat that thinks it belongs up a tree. The credits rolled, the orchestral score died away, and the Rego logo faded to black. Sophie cleared their vision to speak at them.

"I'm sure we can all agree, that was powerful, wonderful, *inspirational* stuff. It makes you think, doesn't it? About who we are, where we belong, and the danger we face when we don't accept things for the way they should be," she said, back in character, posture stiff, voice stern, gaze unflinching – the shrivelled tumour of self-loathing raging against her unending fight to remain professional. "You have the best part of a day to learn how to behave like Tops for the camera. You should all feel very excited and honoured."

After putting away the seats, Sophie lined the clients up outside A-suite and let herself in. A waif of a man was standing in the centre of the room, muttering to himself. His ridiculously short trousers, exposing ridiculously patterned socks, was all she needed to see to know he had no business looking after her twelve monsters.

"Mrs. Burns! I know who you are because I have looked at a lot of pictures of you. I'm Zachary Noblie-Goggins," he poked a thin, pasty arm out from the rolled-up sleeve of his coat and skipped towards her like a puppy. The handshake was clammy. "Sorry... it's sweat. Nothing else... I haven't even been to the toilet today… although, urine is quite sterile. Funny story, did you know it used to be used as mouthwash? By civilised cultures as well, the Romans! Not just some Umbongo tribe."

"Informative," Sophie said as she slipped her hand loose.

"Sorry," he said. "I'm nervous. I've never done this before… speak, I mean… to people. Honestly, though, how hard can it be? Teaching? Just like dog training I expect, except I'll probably be scooping a little more poo… just kidding… I just need to talk to them on their level, no big words, the odd naughty joke, maybe a smidgen of attitude… you feel me?" he laughed.

"I'm *so* pleased they sent you," Sophie said.

"Thank you," he replied, oblivious to her tone. "I'm pleased you're here. I thought I might have to do this alone, but it is nice to be in the company of a professional. Who knows, maybe you'll learn a thing or two! I've prepared a stirring, rip-roaring, gut-punch of a lesson. What I lack in experience, I make up for with hard work… *labor omnia vincit*!" He wore a smug smirk, awaiting admiration. Sophie remained stony-faced – she wasn't in the mood to give this grown child a treat.

"Mr. Noblie-Goggins, you *will* be alone. I was told I was being sent someone qualified. I have a meeting to attend."

Zach stared, statue still, then his tight little mouth started twitching.

"Oh… but… I'm a scientist… not a teacher. And these are Subs. They're animals!" he started hyperventilating. "I can't do this! Don't leave me with them. This is wrong."

"I couldn't agree with you more," Sophie resisted the urge to slap him steady, choosing instead to attempt sympathy. "Unfortunately, this is where we find ourselves. You will be fine. I will stay with you to get them settled and I'll return as soon as I am able. Just remain professional. Don't smile. Blackout their Halos as soon as possible. And don't let *them* hear you call them animals."

When the Subs charged in, Zach's jaw visibly dropped. When he started speaking, Sophie had to blur her vision. She wanted to give the illusion she was looking, but she couldn't bear to watch – his shifty demeanour and rambling voice, the fidgeting of his slender fingers – his very presence was grating. The Subs smirked. It was like watching a lamb trying to lecture wolves. She was thrilled when Dean started misbehaving, she needed an excuse to get out. Her tummy couldn't take the shouting needed to help Zach keep order. His drooped stance made it look like he was already halfway to collapsing, offering his neck to their jaws. Sophie had realised, on the frequent occasions when left with a member of staff who was out of their depth, the best thing for her sanity was to get as far away as possible before the slaughter. She gave Dean a warning she knew he would ignore and went to call her mother. She walked to reception to use the office phone for the privacy of a quiet room.

"Mum, Dean is bloody disgusting," Sophie said.

"Well hello to you too. What the pissing hell do you want me to do about it?"

"Anything, for a start. He's getting worse. I can't keep turning a blind eye, it *really* makes me look incompetent.

The only way down for a Sub is delabelling. Do you have any idea what that would mean for him?"

"Oh, piss off with your bloody Subs and labels. That's your nephew you're talking about."

"Exactly, Mum. And that is the only reason he's still a Rego client. But if he messes up again, that's it. Do you have any idea how important today is for me?"

"He promised he'd be good. What else can I do? I've been excited about the broadcast all week. All the Bingo girls know about it. I want this just as much as you – it's me who looks after him, in case you've forgotten."

"Don't pissin' start. I don't have the bloody energy," Sophie said, dropping into the tatty accent she worked so hard to conceal. "Just do me a favour and stay at home today."

"No. I can't. I've got a leaflet delivery. If I lose the fee for that gig, it'll be a choice between pouches or bingo next week. I'm *not* missing bingo."

"I'll buy your pouches to make up the difference. Bloody hell, I'll buy you some proper food instead."

"Piss off. Don't be so bloody rude. You think buying him a computer system and some broccoli makes it all better. We don't want it. Besides, I can't cancel, my rating's low enough."

"Fine... I'll come by tonight and drive. Help you deliver. Just stay at home, *please*. I've got a few things I need to take care of, but the little... bastard thinks he's so clever, he's going to sneak out, I know it. Ring me if he comes home. I need him involved. It will change him. This *will* make it better."

"On one condition... stop by for tea tonight after we've been out. We never see you anymore. He needs you around. You remind him of his mum."

"Don't bloody insult me," Sophie said. "The boy hates me."

"Just come round."

"We'll see."

Sophie hung up. An evening in the car with her mother! She owed every stoic sinew in her body to that rough, old bird, but a few hours alone with her was more than anyone could stand. She looked out of the reception window and saw Tom Brown fumbling at the car park gate. She'd always liked him. Not enough of a go-getter for the top floor, and too self-righteous, but he was a nice man. It was why she had put her foot down about not letting them sack him. She was grateful they'd listened to her for once and pleased he was back.

After a brief tour, she took Tom up to the Bridge and whizzed through their meeting. Reciting the sickly lines from the Bridge script had been more difficult than usual. Creating an 'environment free from judgement to encourage honest expression' is hard when a grown man weeps. It was Tom's fragility that confirmed he didn't belong above the second floor. He was a wimp. It was embarrassing.

Sophie was ready to escort Tom back to his room so he could sniffle privately when a scream filled the corridor. Sophie knew screams. Years of roaming had honed her ear. She could tell from the pitch whether she was running to break up a fight, or an induction year client was being dunked into a toilet, or a group of Subs was playing Corridor Riot – this scream was different.

Dickie stumbled around the corner and staggered up to Sophie, beads of sweat popping out of the creased, pale skin above the wisps of hair circling his head. He grabbed her elbow so tightly that she pulled away in pain.

"Something has gone wrong," he hissed into her ear. "This is serious. We need to get out now and get this under control, or you are finished. I knew appointing a woman was a mistake."

Zach appeared, covered in blood. Sophie watched in horror as he collapsed into Tom's arms. And then someone else, Sophie had to squint to recognise her – Sally Simon. Classification year, first attempt. Client label, Sub. Demoted from Low for severe insolence and refusal to repent following relocation. Sophie knew she was not a violent girl, the GM from Sally's old site had assured her – she was a filthy, Godless trollop, but never violent.

"What's happened? What's wrong with Sally? *What's happened?*" Sophie whispered. Dickie shook his red face so violently that his chin kept disappearing into his flapping neck. She squeezed his elbow. "What about Dean. Is he OK? *WHERE IS DEAN?*"

"None of them are OK. They're bloody mad!"

Sophie wanted to scream at the pompous oaf, but she saw Tom suddenly kick Sally in the chest, and the other Subs burst onto the corridor from the middle stairwell.

Drowning in the noise filling her head, everything blurred. Somehow, she helped bundle Zach into the Bridge and get the door shut, then she flashed through the broken images of snarling faces that had been running towards her. She hadn't seen Dean. She noticed a large piece of glass sticking out of Zach's back as the gravity of the situation crashed down.

Dickie bent over and wheezed, "If this gets out, you're finished. Get that in your thick skull. Finished!"

Sophie rubbed at the twinge of ache in her tummy, but quickly pulled her hand away again. Now was not the time for Dickie to realise she was pregnant.

7

"UNDER CONTROL"

Tom waited as Zach carefully rolled onto his side. He managed to prop himself up but immediately dropped back into Sophie's lap with the effort.

"What do you mean, turn them off?" Tom said.

"Exactly what I said. What don't you understand? Aren't you a teacher?" Zach said with a pained titter, his eyes darting towards Dickie, as if seeking some gesture of approval. "We need *my* Block. It's in A-suite, under the desk, but locked, so you need to bring it back so I can unlock it. Then we turn *them* off."

"Why not just use another Block?"

"What a brilliant idea!" Zach said. "Why didn't I think of that? Oh, yes, because I'm not stupid. *O me miserum*! Is it any wonder Dr. Vaneman has his work cut out with staff like you?" he glanced at Dickie again and this time was rewarded with a thumbs-up and a nod, so he beamed proudly. "Another Block won't work. Only mine has the programme."

"Who turned *them* on?" Tom ignored Dean's chuckle, "Who's done this?"

"Nobody." Dickie gripped Sophie's shoulder before she could answer. "They're *Subs*. This is what *they* do. But Zach is saying we might get a handle on this hoo-ha if you step up and go and collect his Block."

"Brilliant, so I just stroll out the room, pop downstairs, hunt for the Block, nip back up, all the while avoiding the gang of Subs, get him to unlock the Block, and *then* 'turn them off!' That simple, is it?"

"No," Zach shook his head. "You can't turn them off up here, it's a no-phone area. You need to be on the ground floor."

"Even better. So, after you unlock your screen, I wander out into the corridor and politely ask them all to follow me down the stairs."

"Yes," Zach said.

"Nope. Not going to happen," Tom pinched the bridge of his nose. "This isn't going to work. Not a chance."

"Why not just go back through the room Dean was in?" Ren whispered, mustering a teary smile.

Tom paused, still too bitter to grant Ren the gift of his approval

"Just go back through the room I was in," Dean said.

Tom jumped to his feet, opened the cupboard door, and pointed. "Yes! I'll climb through that!" he said, grabbing Dean's arm and shaking him with excitement. "I'll go out of the other room's door, the Subs might not even hear me, and I'll make a run for it. As soon as I get downstairs, I'll ring the authorities." Tom tried to step into the cupboard but was pulled back by Dickie. Tom elbowed his hand away, "Don't you fucking dare!" he said, snarling as he jabbed his finger into Dickie's face. "Whatever you have been up to, whatever has happened here. I don't care. I'm going downstairs, and I'm ringing the Crusaders. Not Rego, not Drexler, *the Crusaders*. Right after I've broken through that wall." He ran at the cupboard wall, kicking just below the hole. His ankle twisted into the plaster, his knee jolted upwards, and he fell backwards into a shelf.

"Fucking gimp!" Dean said, erupting with laughter.

Tom grasped the ragged plaster edges of the hole and started pulling away chunks like a clumsy child trying to unwrap a present. He exposed two vertical wooden planks and started kicking one, but he collapsed in a heap, defeated.

Dean walked into the cupboard, still laughing, "Move over, shitty shoes."

"It's no use – I'm older than you and I couldn't budge it," Tom said. "I'll just squeeze through the hole if you give me a leg up?"

Dean stared at Tom, insulted, then shooed him away with his hand. He steadied himself by grabbing one of the wooden studs, then started to stamp against the other. He drove his foot into the joist as if possessed, his leg a jackhammer, never slowing. His taut face shook as he rammed his foot. The slamming changed pitch as the wood splintered. He snapped through the timber, then thrust an arm into the cavity and ragged away a slab of wall, bringing an avalanche of rubble crashing to the floor. Dean heaved out enough angry breaths to force any emotion back under before turning around and giving his mandatory laugh.

"You should be able to manage the rest, limp dick."

Early in Tom's suspension, he'd been included in a staff email chain demanding Dean be relocated after beating a kid senseless. They were calling for an end to the favouritism towards this dangerous client. Tom had thought the teachers were using a common playground fight as an excuse to attack Sophie – she *was* wildly unpopular – but watching Dean demolish that wall, Tom could well imagine the damage he'd cause with that dead rage. Someone with all that bubbling beneath can't be trusted.

Tom walked through to the adjoining room and Dean followed.

"What are you doing?" Tom said.

"I'm coming," he replied.

"What? No, you're not. Get back in the other room."

"Dean. Come in here *now*," Sophie hissed. "*Dean*, come back at once… please."

He peered through the hole and looked back at his aunt, "No," he said.

"You need to stay with me, so I can keep you safe."

Dean laughed. "Fuck off. Stop pretending you give a shit."

"Of course I do," she said, swallowing back the threat of tears.

His top lip curled, "Stop being a wimp, it's embarrassing! Stop pretending you're bothered about anyone else. You limpet on to me because all you've got is a bored husband who shags every Janet forced into his office. I'm the fucking... cute, little, poor example, that proves you're not an empty, sour *cunt!* No-one's fooled."

"Oh, Dean," she sighed. "Please don't leave. Please know I want you with me." But he'd stopped listening.

"Look, shitty sho- Mr. Brown, Sir," Dean said. "You call the authorities on a bunch of Subs, they'll drag me in just for being here. I'm following you down, and I'm going."

Dickie squeezed out a deliberate cough. He had pushed through to join them and was covered in brick dust and bits of rubble, his ruddy, wrinkled forehead beaded with sweat from the effort.

"Tom, a word, please."

Tom walked over and was greeted with the grin of a deviant offering jelly drops from a moist paper bag.

"Maybe I wasn't clear," Dickie said. "There will be *no* phoning of the Crusaders. The best option is for you to ring the switchboard, and in the meantime, see if we can't get these... *things* under control. Anything else and we run the risk of people getting hurt." His voice was soft, the smile starting to expose teeth. "Think of the Subs... those clients out there... they all matter. *Even* the Subs. If you resort to informing the authorities, instead of handling this in-house, they will certainly be delabelled. Their families will be relocated. And a lifetime of working the Lines, at best. I *know* their behaviour is abhorrent, but they deserve forgiveness. They deserve a second chance."

"I knew I hated you," Tom said. "Those awful broadcasts. That... voice – thanking God for all the good he's let you do for the Nation. It's so transparent. What a sad sign of how useless we all are that people like you succeed. The malicious, shit-stirring cowards who'd kick the women and children off lifeboats. I bet this won't even matter anyway. Whatever you've done, you'll hide. You'll be on the next broadcast with miraculous news about national client progress or some new sodding way of getting the miserable shits to smile and recite... fuck you."

"I'll finish you," Dickie said quickly. He still had a strange little smile stuck on his face but his eyes had narrowed.

"What?" Tom said, startled.

"You *will* come back upstairs with that Block, or I'll finish you. I know why you were suspended, you filthy little man. You'd be surprised at how many times your name has been on the agenda. You've been quite the headache. You're right, whatever this is, I'll deal with it. You, however, will be finished. It will be my pleasure to make sure of it. The last thing Rego needs is to try and stand in support of a teacher who wouldn't restrain himself in the company of a pretty little girl."

Tom clenched his teeth so tightly he almost choked, "*But it was a lie.*"

"Once you are done having to explain the sticky details of the sordid accusation, I think people will start to get a little tired of hearing your excuses. You'll never teach again.

I guarantee it. Oh, don't worry though, I'll see to it you can work elsewhere, a nice little job cleaning toilets somewhere. Is that what you want to make me do to you? Now... do the right thing. For the clients."

Tom slammed his fist into Dickie's floppy throat. It was the first time he had ever hit anyone. Dickie stumbled into a desk and clutched at his neck. Tom stalked forward and grabbed him by the collar, his shaking fist raised.

"...Go on! Hit him again!" Dean said, sitting on the edge of a desk, sucking his Regovape and grinning. "Come on! Slap him... go on... kill him!"

Tom pressed his knuckles into Dickie's big cheek, Dickie closed his eyes and tried to turn away.

"... Go on... fucking slap him!" Dean was twitching for bloodshed. "Knock the fucker out!"

Tom pressed his forehead into Dickie's ear and blasted out an angry breath, but his moment had passed, he could feel himself softening.

"... aww, come on, pussy!" Tom unclenched his hand and stepped away. Dean rolled his eyes, "That's the gayest fight I've ever seen. I'm surprised you didn't end up wanking him off."

"I'm going," Tom said.

Dean picked up a loose textbook and frisbeed it at Dickie's gut, then followed Tom out.

"Do the right thing, Mr. Brown," Dickie said, still clutching his neck. "Do you hear me? Tom? TOM?"

Tom stepped out into the corridor. He thought about peering around the corner to look at the Subs hammering the Bridge door, but Dean had already walked through to the top of the West stairwell. All was silent apart from the distant thudding. They picked up speed, skipping down groups of stairs at a time, confident that all the Subs were on the top floor. On the ground, Dean walked straight past the A-suite, but Tom stopped and pulled out his phone.

"Dean," he hissed. "Wait there. I'm ringing."

Dean jogged back to Tom, bobbing his head, unable to contain a genuine hint of wide-eyed excitement, clearly thrilled at the prospect of Crusaders storming the site, booting down the doors and smashing in Dickie's skull before their shared brain cell realised who he was – a fantasy Tom appreciated. The privatisation of the Nation's policing spawned the Civility And Peace Enforcement unit (CAPE). A force made up of 'proud and patriotic' volunteers, rewarded with a steady supply of RegoJolt (typically reserved for body-conscious Villagers) to compensate for their pouch-fed physiques. After a number of high-profile incidents, the broadcasts started referring to CAPE as the Crusaders in an attempt to rebrand their blunt brutality.

Dean leaned in to listen for an idea of when to expect some aimless caped Crusader fury.

"I'm on hold," Tom said, his voice quivering with nerves. He put a finger to his lips. "... Yes... could I be put through to Mr. Drexler, please? It's an emergency," Dean stopped bobbing as his excitement drained away. Tom raised his eyes to the ceiling to avoid his judgemental stare. "Mr. Drexler? Is this Mr. Drexler?" Tom said.

"Speaking," he replied.

"Hello, I'm Tom Brown. Mr. Brown of site 102. Dr.Vaneman told me to contact you."

"... ..."

"It's the Subs. They've lost it. We need to turn them off, or something, I don't know. I was told to ring you." Embarrassed by Dean's disappointment, he started shouting, "Look, unless you do something here, I'm going to ring the authorities. I mean it. I know you don't want to hear that, but believe me, if you can't help, I'll ring them. Everyone is trapped in a room upstairs. They're safe, but one of your guys, Zach, he's in a bad way. He's been stabbed. He could die. And the Subs are tearing themselves apart. What are you going to do about it?"

"Where is Vaneman?"

"He's locked upstairs!"

"Zach?"

"Him too. He's bad! He's got a lump of glass hanging out his back. Now, tell me, what are you going to do?"

"A team will be there."

"When? And what do I do until then?" Tom said. "What team?" but there was no answer. Tom finally met Dean's stare. "They're sending a team... ringing the company was the right thing. They are the best people to handle this... it was the right thing to do."

"Whatever," Dean said, turning to walk towards the main entrance.

"Don't phone the Crusaders," Tom said. "Don't. Your aunt will lose her job. All your friends will be delabelled. Don't phone them."

"I wasn't goin' to."

"... You're a good kid. I know most don't think so, but I always liked you. Back before you lost your mother," Dean's shoulders flickered a shrug of recognition, "when you'd just started, I always enjoyed teaching you. You were much smarter than all the others. I can't imagine what you've been through. I'm going back up and I could do with your help, but I understand if you need to run away."

"Bye, shitty shoes," Dean continued walking.

Tom stared into the A-suite camera and opened the door. Broken glass littered the room, and there were scattered desktops and stray chair legs covering the floor. The touchwall was on a loop of Sophie reciting the fundamental values, her body rippled and discoloured by a crack that zigzagged the width of the wall. Tom stepped over the puddles and blood spots and looked under the desk.

He picked up the smooth, clear cube and unfolded it like an old map until the width filled his stretched arms. A picture of a lock pulsed in the centre of the large screen. He folded it back down until it sat neatly on his hand, the lock symbol now a tiny throbbing light on a small transparent square, and slipped it into his pocket.

He stepped out of the room and looked outside at Dean with a pang of envy – he could join him out there and end this. But Tom knew it was a fantasy. He knew he would go running upstairs with his tail tucked. He had spent the last three years of his marriage fantasising about waking up alone, but the day his wife had finally left, he'd begged her to stay like a blubbing child. Since the Nation's ministers had focused their piety on education, and turned schools into sites and students into clients, the remnants of what Tom still enjoyed about his arse-end of a career had shriveled away like strangled polyps. For so long he pined for something else, to be something else. But the moment Dickie had threatened to take it all away, he felt like he was grasping at his wife's ankles again. Outside, Dean was nonchalantly puffing out thick white clouds above his head. *It's easy to be brave when you've no responsibility.*

He walked back to the stairwell and quietly made his way up to the third floor. He walked through the double doors when he was sure the corridor was empty. He could hear the steady thud around the corner. He got to the door of the adjoining room and his stomach plummeted as he stared at the camera box and realised he didn't have Top access. He peered through the narrow window in the door. There was a direct line of sight all the way through to the Bridge. Tom squeezed his fist as he tapped the glass, as if tensing would add volume to his tiny knocks. Dickie sauntered past the open cupboard door and Tom flailed his arms, skipping on the spot to try and grasp his attention. He winced as he allowed his knock to get louder. Dickie appeared again, his big back filling the cupboard opening. Tom listened for the steady thud around the corner, and after five echoed bangs, he timed his heavy knock with the sixth. Dickie's back slowly swiveled and Tom waved furiously. Dickie waddled towards him.

"No! Please run away!" sobbed a gentle voice. Tom shot a glance at a scrawny, little Sub, peering at him through his wet, flopped fringe.

Tom turned back to the door and slammed his fists against it. Dickie fumbled and squeezed his wide frame through the hole. The Sub screamed and ran at Tom, who ducked, sending the boy toppling over. Dickie dived at the handle, opening the door, and Tom fell into the room, but as he tried to push it shut, the boy jumped side first into the gap, squeezing his head and chest in. He grabbed Tom's sleeve in his teeth, ripping at material as he shook his jaw from side to side. He spat thread from his mouth and begged Tom to run away. Dickie barged into the door, crunching it into the boy's ribs, who pleaded for it to stop, before shooting his hand up to grab Tom's ear. The skin on the side of Tom's face seared as the boy tried to tear it away. The sound of feet came galloping from around the corner.

"They're all coming!" Dickie shouted. "Get a ruddy move on, you useless man!"

Tom yanked his head away and Dickie rammed the door a second time. The boy wheezed and spluttered, then raked his nails down Dickie's face.

"Let him in!" Tom shouted. "We need to shut this door, pull him in."

The sudden shift from pushing to pulling took the boy by surprise and he flew into the room, clattering into a bookcase. Dickie shut the door as a barrage of bloodied hands started hammering the narrow window.

"What's happening?" Sophie shouted from the other room. Ren poked her face through the hole, looked at the Sub on the floor, and disappeared with a burst of tears.

"You've done… something to my… chest. It hurts." The boy spoke between rasping breaths. "Please… stop. Help me."

And then he lurched forward. He was small, but his strength was unrestrained. Tom fell backward onto the floor, underneath the Sub's desperate clawing. As the boy started jerking his head up and down, he butted straight into Tom's nose. Dickie scooped the boy up by his armpits and launched him back into the bookcase.

Tom managed to stand up and smear away the blood and spit from his nose with the back of his hand. The boy paused again for a few more strained breaths, then he lowered himself onto all fours.

"I'm sorry," he said. "I don't know what I'm doing."

"He's not going to stay down," Tom said. "And if we keep going, we'll kill him."

"Please stop," the boy sobbed.

"The extension cable, in the cupboard, wrap him in it," Dickie whispered.

Dickie backed towards the cupboard. The boy gave him a twitchy glance, then bolted at Tom, scurrying on his hands and feet, ramming headfirst into his chest. Dickie bundled the boy off Tom and flipped him onto his stomach. Without time to think, he dropped his full weight on the child, covering his tiny frame and muffling his screams.

Tom ran to the cupboard, grabbed the extension cable, and looped it around his hand and elbow until he had a thick handful of hoops. Dickie thrust his hands under the boy's chin and pulled his head back, bending his face up to the ceiling. Tom slid the cable over the boy's head and pushed it down his body, over his arms, and tugged it tight.

It took a sweaty bout of rolling and fumbling, always avoiding the boy's snapping jaws, before he was forced onto a seat and wrapped in the remaining cable, then two full rolls of sticking tape were unravelled around him to fasten him tight. The boy kept writhing against the restraints, briefly pausing for calm, before returning to confined frenzy.

*   *   *

Sophie carefully picked at a blood clot that had knotted a clump of Zach's hair. She was a picture of calm. It was a delicate forgery.

At least once, every single day since her sister's first suicide attempt, Sophie wrestled with a seething panic. She'd close her eyes and breath through the tsunami rather than bludgeon her husband, or a client, or some stranger who happened to pick the wrong moment to stare. Since Dean had followed Tom out, breathing was not quelling *this* tsunami. It was when Dean was his most vicious that her heart *really* ached, stripped of his conscious effort to shock, the hatred uncontrived. She mourned every moment she'd ever told the scared boy to suck it up. Her misery had made her dismiss his, so she witnessed his steady decline into the rancid bastard of a boy he had become. It's the frail deception of weak adults that turns children into what they are.

The chaos from the adjoining room became too loud to ignore. Sophie stood up, pushed her head through the plaster gap, and looked at the beaten child tied to a chair – *Casey*

Richardson. Assessment Year 2, first attempt. Client label, Sub. Demoted from Top to Sub after grave sin, possession of weapon and refusal to repent.

"Shit," she muttered. She always thought of Casey as a polite boy who never should have been demoted. He had no business being a Sub. She'd offered him CTRL in a pathetic attempt to make amends, like giving an infant a lolly after flattening its kitten under your tyre, hoping to stifle the wails before anyone came running to see what the fuss was about. Casey Richardson did not deserve to be in that chair. His tiny body shimmered with reams of tape. Through the sobbing exhaustion, his eyes kept rolling backward as his sodden head drooped. Smears of blood, old and new, flecked his body like paint, there was no way of knowing how much of it was his.

"We have to get a move on. Because this," she pointed at Casey, "is an ugly fuc... flipping look for us."

*   *   *

Dean watched as Tom walked down the corridor to the stairwell and then disappeared. He knew Mr. Brown was a streak of piss, but he'd let himself believe the teacher *would* ring the Crusaders. He would've loved sitting on the other side of the street, hidden away, watching them surround the site, before marching that fat, bumbling, Dickie prick into the back of a panel van. His aunt would slither her filth up to his sweaty lap so she could suck out one last promotion and finally move to a village where she belonged, away from him. Dean's gut ached with hate.

After his mum killed herself, for a while he felt nothing. Eventually, the tired emptiness filled with bile. He became disgusted by the misery of others. Random road accidents were a chance for him to walk by and smirk at the grief of strangers. He wanted everyone to suffer. He wanted parents crying over stillborn children, trucks flattening crowds, bombs to drop, people to starve, everything to rot.

Her death hadn't been a shock. She'd talked about doing it for a long time, and when her rare happy days disappeared altogether, Dean could make peace with her need to escape. But she hadn't left a note – he wished for some kind of proof that he was at least a passing thought before she'd given up. There was no goodbye. Nothing left behind.

Everybody feigned sadness for a while but soon got bored of asking him if he was OK and him not giving the comfortable answer, so he stopped responding and ignored every fucking one of them. He'd waited six months for the counseling session his aunt had paid for, and after a fifty-minute bus ride to register, he was given an online consultation where he was prescribed an eye-watering subscription to a cocktail of tablets, forcing him to deny that he was ever stupid enough to have hoped that it was going to improve.

His Aunt already expected him to worship her every time she stopped him from getting kicked out of 102, thinking she was saving his life because now and then she'd bring him *real* vegetable soup, or proper apples so Nan could bake his mum's tart. There was no way he was going to let her bankrupt herself for his happy pills. She had begged him to reconsider, blubbing her misty eyes. She hadn't even cried at the funeral. They were the crocodile tears of a selfish bitch. She didn't give a fuck.

He stopped at a plaque, 'Dr. Richard Vaneman, Esq. CEO, BBS, MBS, FUNV' engraved into the gold plating marking a space filled with some shitty two-door. Dean was surprised, he'd have guessed that Vaneman would have had a plush self-drive to compensate for the nub of a cock he probably had hiding under his paunch. He pulled out his house keys and scraped a deep line down the side of the paintwork. He stepped back and smashed his foot into the doors, stamping the bodywork until it wouldn't buckle any further. He rammed a rock against the bonnet, leaving sharp dents in the hood, then smashed it into the windshield, grasping the stone with two hands and crunching it until the fractured glass sagged over the steering wheel. He thumped wildly, his fists slamming, not stopping even as his knuckles bloodied the dented metal. A note fluttered loose from the wiper and struck Dean in the face. He unfolded it and read the contents. He sighed, then flung his rock towards the towering Rego logo above the main entrance - a blocky monument to swallowing every vinegar drip the liars squeezed through your lips, preparing you for a lifetime of quietly scrubbing their floors.

He thought about his aunt, trapped, clinging to her job so she could keep buying her high heels and suit jackets, and he padded at the embarrassing sting in his eyes. He hated her. He fucking *hated* her.

But he needed to make sure she was OK.

8

ZACHARY
NOBLIE-GOGGINS

Zach swallowed deep breaths to calm his panic. He was no stranger to this sensation, anything out of the ordinary would trigger it, but his anxiety was beyond control today. He was preparing to talk to a room of clients. Worse than that, Subs. *This* was out of the ordinary.

Zach actively avoided mixing with anyone from the zones. He lived smack in the centre of North Third Village. It was cheaper than First, and to be perfectly honest, he preferred the Art Deco theme to the Edwardian. He considered himself too young at heart to be enamoured by the quaint stylings of old England. He'd stretched himself to afford his modest two-bed apartment, but it meant he was surrounded by a truly elite crowd. Zach was one of only a few in his tower that worked, most were inheritors, all from great stock, which had upped the price. It was worth it; he got to rub shoulders with the cream, the streaming speed was tremendous, and he was about as far from any zone as you could be (he'd read some truly terrible things).

Yet, when he heard that Dr.Richard Vaneman had personally asked for him to go and assist with the initiation of the CTRL programme, he agreed. He drove straight into the heart of darkness – a zoned estate! How could anyone refuse such a man?

He'd planned a lesson down to the finest detail, having taken a copy of Rego's 'Guide for Outstanding Facilitators' and read it cover to cover. Twice. He'd equipped himself with all manner of resources to 'keep their underdeveloped minds occupied' (according to the guide). He'd scripted the entire thirty-minute session, with answers to a list of questions he was sure would be asked once he'd aroused their curiosity. And he'd also included a great many jokes, some a little risqué, just to keep things fun, as well as educational. He'd arrived at site 102 at seven AM and had already practised the lesson a dozen times. He was in control of his nerves, (just), and with some last-minute prompts scribbled on the inside of his hand, he felt ready.

He couldn't deny he was the product of good genes and a great education. His father had seen to that. But he had always been adamant that it was work ethic and attitude that made the man. When faced with a challenge, he didn't whine, he worked. 'The *only* barrier between a man and his success is elbow grease… *faber est suae quisque fortunae*.' Father had said to him when he had agreed to grant him a modest loan to start his own medical research firm. And Father was right, as always. He worked hard, damned hard, and Rego came sniffing after he'd landed his first contract with an old school chum.

Zach heard idle chatter outside the room, a woman's shriek telling people to 'shut up and stand still,' and he suddenly felt light-headed. He planted his hands on his desk to stop anyone from seeing how much he was shaking. He had sweated through two layers and was starting to moisten the armpits of his lab coat.

Mrs. Burns walked in and introduced herself, then she let the vermin scurry in. Zach's knees weakened. They looked exactly like those boisterous bastards that used to sit at the back of the bus on his way to St Edmunds School for Boys. Even now, the sight of public transport was enough to bring back unsettling echoes of the barbarity of the indolent.

After some mild shenanigans, Mrs. Burns ordered the most outspoken Sub, Dean, out of the suite. The others all stared at Zach – a room of mangled teeth and wrath. Zach seized the opportunity to use his focus ball, a fluffy orb that he could throw as a physical prompt to keep a weak mind engaged (according to the guide). He tossed it to a cock-eyed urchin on the front row.

"What the fuck ya gimme this faggot thing for?" the urchin said, then he hacked a glob from his throat and dripped it into the ball's pink fur before launching it back at Zach's face. The Subs became raucous. Mrs. Burns shoved her head back into the room and started screaming.

After she left, Dean bounced back in to announce he was being sent home. It was the small shred of relief Zach needed.

One fewer to deal with! His spirits lifted. He reminded himself that *he* was the adult in the room, *he* was in charge, *he* was responsible for determining the atmosphere (according to the guide). He was no longer the child sobbing into his briefcase while bus rats pelted him with cherryade-soaked tampons.

"Be quiet!" he shouted. The noise continued, an array of sounds, some words, but mostly squeaks and grunts. They couldn't even talk to each other properly, Zach thought; they were repellent. "Immediately, please... shush, I say. QUIET!" they completely ignored him, like he was making no sound at all. It was bizarre how maddeningly discourteous they were, Zach thought; they were a different breed. "Shush up, now... or I'll tell Mrs. Burns... NOW!" he shouted as he walked over to the door and threatened to open it. To his relief, they gradually quietened.

Instead of launching into his memorised script, Zach decided to adlib a quick intro – something to set the mood, concerned that he may be coming across as a tad despotic, he wanted to let them know it wasn't going to be all work, no play.

"Thank you for being silent," he said. Every one of them was still whispering. "Now that we've rid ourselves of Mrs. Burns... woof... you know what I'm saying... I can be a bit more normal with you guys. We can have a bit of a laugh. You guys have probably worked out that I'm not like a normal teacher... that's because I'm not a teacher. Teachers are crap. Apologies for the potty mouth, but, am I right? Bloody crap! I know I shouldn't say it, but... whoopsie daisies! I'm not much different from you guys. So, if you can stay coolio, so can I."

Zach searched for a smile. There wasn't one. Not to worry, he thought, on with the script. His best material was in that.

"Today, kids, we're going to do a little roleplay… no, not that kind, perverts!" Zach snorted, but none of the Subs reacted. "Not that I doubt your propensity for debauched bacchanalia, I'm sure even a weekday night for some of you would shame Caligula himself!" the room remained silent. His mouth dried. He knew he'd pitched that one too high. "Today you get to star in our Nation's evening broadcast, and not because your dirty Sub backsides are in need of a spanking," no laughter again. He could feel his heart beating in his ears. The panic was filling him too fast to consider changing what he was going to say. "For once you guys have done something right! About bloody time, am I right? You've picked CTRL. It's time to take back control because you vagabonds probably couldn't even do that during your last toilet trip. *Am I right?*" that was his favourite joke, but it was like he was speaking another language – they found *nothing* funny. The thumping embarrassment filled his head. He was back on the bus, pants around his ankles, flopping around trying to cover his shrunken genitals from the pointing and cackling. He just needed to get through his script quickly. He took a deep breath and spoke without pause, "With the help of CTRL I am going to teach you a National Values lesson, be gentle with me it's my first time, I hope it doesn't hurt. Much. And then later on today, we'll do it all over again in front of the cameras. Stop giggling you filthy lot, I mean the lesson – I haven't done *that* twice in one day since some work colleagues pooled together for a birthday surprise! And believe me, there were no cameras involved that day, just a pair of handcuffs, a turkey baster, and an extra-large tub of hummus." His voice started to dwindle, he strained against his disappearing breath, "But enough about me, let's see what we are dealing with before CTRL does its thing. Here's a short video about you. We'll be showing it again later – it's quite unpleasant, so, as the actress said to the bishop, *statum assumat.*" He hammered the button on the touchwall and took a huge gulp with a dry slap of his mouth. The Subs' eyes disappeared behind darkened glass as the video filled their screens.

The speakers shook with the heavy bass of hideous music – a tune the focus group had identified as the most fitting. Accompanying the grimy sound, an image of each Sub appeared on screen, one after the other. Their blank profile picture expressions stared out above a list of their misdemeanours. Each Sub cheered when it was their turn to feature. When Sally Simons' sin of 'Public demonstration of lust' appeared, a 'slag' chant started ringing around the room. She laughed and stuck her middle fingers above her head. The final Sub was Bradley Sherrington. The room hushed as the usual intro cut to recorded footage.

The broadcast team had insisted on the inclusion of the clip – it would be unpatriotic to sugarcoat what *they* are capable of, plus, the people love a little violence. Dr.Vaneman had agreed – 'Let the Nation see the true face of the animals

I'm dealing with, on the front line, every day. So, they can rejoice in the good that I'll bring,' he'd said.

The recording showed Brad at the front of a classroom. The Sub was flinging his arms, displaying like some ape, before unzipping himself and urinating in a bin. Then, when the teacher had tried to stop him, he'd repeatedly slapped her face until she retreated off-screen. The most disturbing thing during the clip's eerie silence was the pixilation around the boy's groin where he hadn't bothered to pull himself back in before assaulting her.

There was a reverential hush. Then unrestrained joy as fists pounded desks and cheers filled the air. Brad acknowledged the appreciation with a nod.

"OK, OK," Zach pleaded. "Settle down. Shush now." But the Subs didn't settle. They started stamping, quicker and quicker. Zach pressed the touchwall button to clear their vision – if they were to respect his rule, it would be with a stern voice and a steely stare (according to the guide). "Settle down, I said hush your mouths," he locked eyes with Brad, and immediately regretted it. What stared back could not be matched. Brad climbed onto his desk, stamping, and conducting the rest of them in violent cheer. Zach had lost them. "Sit down," he said. "Please. Sit. You animals. Please." The guide had no advice for this. He looked at the sweat-blurred notes on his hand and continued talking quietly, drowned out by the madness. "We all know what you are – but CTRL will change that. Your focus, your judgem…" A pen flung towards Zach, but he instinctively dodged. "Your judgement. Your emotional maturity. They are all traits that have led you down your ugly path because you can't control yourselves." Another pen came flying. The chatter and chants and laughter spiraling, a maddening tinnitus filling Zach with helpless rage. "Shush. Just shush. Shut up!" he said, a little louder. "Please. Shut up." Another pen flipped through the air and struck his cheek. "SHUT UP! MONGREL BASTARDS. YOU FILTHY, ROTTEN, ZONE RAT, SUB BASTARDS. JUST SHUT YOUR DIRTY LITTLE BASTARD MOUTHS. SHUT UP! SHUT UP! *SHUT UP!*" They stared. He panted, then slammed the touchwall button to re-block their vision. Brad, blinded, stumbled on his desk and clattered to the floor.

"... What the fuck did you just call us?" snarled a Sub.

Zach's shuddering breath cut through the simmering. The door clicked. Dr.Vaneman stood at the entrance, staring curiously at the stand-off.

"Everything tip-top in here?" he asked.

"Well... wow!" stuttered Zach. The nerves shook a drop of sweat from the tip of his nose. "Just wow! What a privilege for us all." He started clapping as he filled with a desperate mix of fear and elation, overjoyed to finally be in the presence of the man he'd admired for so long, dizzyingly sick that this was the moment being witnessed. "It's so special to have you here, Sir. I was just telling the Subs about today. We are just getting to know each other. These guys are almost as crazy as me! We are having a great laugh. Aren't we Subs?"

Brad stood up. "Give me back my fucking sight so I can *fucking KILL YOU!*"

Zach stared at Dr.Vaneman and whimpered, his bottom lip quivering. "I'm sorry, Sir."

Chairs scraped as every Sub took determined steps towards the sound of Zach's voice. Some swiped arms, daring him to repeat himself.

"What on God's green earth is going on in here?" Dr.Vaneman fixed Zach with a disgusted stare, daring him to look away.

"It's the Subs, Sir. They're animals," Zach said. The Subs responded with a cacophony of dissent. Zach gestured at their booing and cursing as proof. Still blind, they moved forward again, clawed hands outstretched, the anger growing. Zach stumbled back until he was by the CEO's side.

"Go out into the corridor, so we don't all have to suffer your whimpering," Dr.Vaneman said to Zach. Zach didn't hesitate. "Calm down, all of you. I will be with you shortly. I'll get to the bottom of this, trust me," Dr.Vaneman said to the Subs, then he slammed the door behind him as they started kicking at whatever blocked their sightless hounding.

Zach was bent over, keeping himself steady by gripping his knees. "I'm sorry, Dr.Vaneman, Sir. They just lost it in there, I have no idea why."

Dr.Vaneman rubbed Zach's back. "Calm down, man. You're making a fool of yourself. I'm sure it's nothing I can't fix."

"Thank you, Sir. Thank you… it's an honour to finally meet you. I've worked tirelessly to make sure everything will run smoothly today. I was hoping to make you proud."

"And proud I hope to be if you can stop blubbing. Now, come on, pull yourself together. Mrs. Burns will be down shortly, how am I expected to get through today with *two* women by my side? I expect you to be the glue that holds this place together."

"You are an inspiration, Sir," Zach said, the panic drifting away, slightly giddy from Dr.Vaneman's tone, like he was being granted one of his father's pep talks, elated there wasn't a hint of disgust. "I was about to start the first practice run of the lesson. They need to rehearse so they can conduct themselves in a manner that best showcases our impact. Remove the variables."

"You take a moment out here to calm yourself. You've embarrassed yourself enough for one day. I'll start the lesson. Join me when you're ready." Dr.Vaneman stood Zach up, gave his shoulders a warm squeeze, then walked back in and shut the door.

Zach stepped away from the muffled shouting and composed himself. They were monsters. If anything, the leaflets and broadcasts had underplayed the crisis. Having witnessed these degenerates first hand, he could imagine the carnage if a handful entered a village. It wasn't enough for Zach that the brainless bullies that ruined his childhood now lived miles away, crammed into their flats, squeezing out their spawn by the dozen. Because, despite the steady disappearance of their grubby dissent over the years, there was still never more than a day between riots - protesting because it's easier to complain than to do an honest day's work. And now that Zach had seen their rage first hand, he understood just how dangerous *they* could be. Something had to be done, he thought. Since the Ministers had taken charge, after all the doubts about the Nation's potential, they couldn't allow mercy for the mindless to halt progress. All the advances and initiatives that removed the pointless protection for the apathetic – stripping the clutter of regulation had done *so* much good for people that wanted to knuckle down. Life in the village was paradise. But these… *Subs!* They could tear it all down.

"Excuse me! You there," Dr. Vaneman said, knocking on the glass. "Get in here, now."

Zach ran in. The Subs were all grunting, their heads slumped. The sound reminded Zach of the strange corner of the fitness centre in his complex, filled with Jolted young men swinging weights as he clocked up his minutes on the cross-trainer.

"I'm not moving!" Sally screamed.

Dr. Vaneman looked furious. "What's wrong?" he asked. "What did you do?"

"*Me?*… *I* didn't *do* anything. Other than fixing your mess as you sobbed outside," Dr. Vaneman pulled a face as if he'd just stuck his nose in something rancid. "Now fix this, or do I need to get someone down here who knows what they are doing?"

"*No!*" Zach's mouth was so dry that it felt like he was trying to spit his words through sand. "No. NO. I can do this. I'll make it right. I know what the problem is."

Zach didn't know what the problem was. He snatched his Block back and opened the CTRL app, ignoring whether the fluttering in his chest was what a heart attack felt like.

Sally clawed at the goggles sucked to her face. Zach ran towards her and held his Block up to unlock the strap before she pulled her eyes from their sockets. The other Subs started to try and tear their Halos away, so he sprinted to the touch-wall and jabbed at the button to clear their vision. Their eyes appeared and their grunts silenced. They looked around the room, as if seeing for the first time – a deep breath after being submerged.

Sally picked up the jug of orange cordial from the refresh-ment trolley and threw it against the floor, spreading juice and glass everywhere. Zach tossed his Block under the desk, so he had both hands free, and ran towards her. The Subs took a long breath in unison. He grabbed Sally by the hand and slowly stepped her out from between the scattered glass before she hurt herself. She paused, jolting back Zach's hand. Suddenly, with a guttural shriek, the Subs all jumped onto their desks, some on all fours.

"... You've got to run," Sally whispered. "We're going to hurt you."

"Pardon?" said Zach.

"Run!" she screamed. She dropped her hands to the floor, picked up a long dagger of glass, and slashed at Zach's stomach, slicing just above his bony hip. He stumbled into the centre of the suite, only for all the other Subs to launch at him. Fingers scratched and scraped, feet and fists rained down. Zach looked towards the door as he heard it slam shut,

Dr.Vaneman had disappeared. Sally pounced through the gang of attackers, landing on Zach's back. He spun around underneath her so she was on his chest and she dug her left hand into his throat. She moved in fits of jerking speed, but her face was soft, crying. And she kept apologising.

Zach bucked his hips and she toppled to the side. The clients carried on kicking, but Zach scurried back across the room, through the juice and glass, underneath a cluster of desks. They went for him, flinging chairs and tables across the room. There was no focus to their pursuit, pausing to kick and smash at anything in their way.

Zach scurried out from under his mound and kicked a desk towards the gang. Its metal feet scraped across the floor before bashing into their legs. They pounced at the table like a pack of strays. He barged a scrawny Sub out of the way, knocking him against a wall, and ran out of the room. Dr.Vaneman looked startled. He was standing in the middle of the corridor with his Block in hand, mid dial. Zach ran towards him and dragged him through the West stairwell doors just as the Subs burst out of the suite. They stuck their noses in the air and looked around. Zach ducked below the door's window, and when he finally peered back, they were all tearing down the East corridor.

"They're gone," he said.

"Good," said Dr.Vaneman. "They're bloody animals. I need to make a call. Sort these crazies out. Don't worry, I'll go on record to state that, as far as I could tell, this wasn't entirely your fault." He placed his hands on Zach's shoulders and gave them a squeeze.

"Quick. I'll walk you to reception, Sir."

Dr. Vaneman wiped his bloodied hand on Zach's coat and opened the door to let him lead the way. "Call me Dickie."

Suddenly, Sally clattered headfirst into Zach's chest. Dickie didn't hesitate – he turned and started leaping up the stairs, three at a time.

She held the tip of her glass shard against Zach's shoulder and turned her face away from having to watch as she rammed it in, pushing until it scraped bone. Drawing on a strength taken from his agony, Zach grasped Sally's hand and squeezed until her fingers cracked, then slowly pulled the glass out. He swivelled his shoulder and let her slam her force into the floor, then he shoved her away and ran.

By the time he'd dragged himself up to the top floor, his shoulder and stomach were pulsing, a sensation he'd experienced once before. His last school bus journey (and the reason his father had finally relented and arranged for alternative transport) had involved a progression of sorts for his bus bullies. They moved from ridicule with a dash of light battery, to serious assault, when one thumped a utility knife into his tummy. He still had digestion issues after a piece of his small intestine had to be removed. Being stabbed, Zach realised, did not become more bearable with familiarity. He collapsed into the open arms of some man and locked eyes with Dickie, who looked unharmed, safe, all thanks to his selfless intervention. A tingle of pride briefly masked his pain. Then, he felt a sharp, searing pressure in his back. And all went dark.

9

"YOU HAVE TO FIX THIS"

Ren wept silently, hunched and rocking in a corner, like a nudged vase.

"Ren, I know you're scared. We all are. But you really ought to pull yourself together," Sophie was directing her brand of compassion elsewhere in Dean's absence. "We need all the help we can get. Come on."

"You don't need me," Ren said. "Leave me alone."

"Stop crying! Your attitude is making it worse. Be positive. We'll be fine! We just need a bit of belief," Sophie's eyes drifted towards the ceiling as if she were talking to herself more than Ren. "Come on! Up! Help me out, what can we do here?"

"Nothing. There's nothing I can do," Ren said. "There's nothing I want to do. Nothing's going to change."

"Ren, I don't need change. No one can change anything at the moment, but we can adapt our outlook. Make the best of a bad situation. Come on, you used to be such a strong, little girl."

"GOD!" Ren shouted. Then, for a moment, the tears stopped and she screamed. A long, fierce noise. Then a pause, "Don't call me a girl! Leave me alone. I'm not smiling this away. Ignore me. Keep concentrating on being a nodding accomplice to that fat puddle of a boss, who you so clearly despise."

"... OK! Fine!" The silence bristled until it seemed Sophie could hold her tongue no longer. "It's a sad state of affairs how far you've let yourself fall, you know. You were a great client, bags of potential, ready to turn into a promising young woman. It's not so bleak out there, a girl with the right attitude can go far. It's all about how you handle your situation. Right now, this is a test. Apply yourself and you'll succeed. Use this as an opportunity to start afresh. Look at me, we're not so different. With a change of attitude, there's no reason why you can't get to where I am."

Ren shook her head slowly enough to be sincerely patronising, "Excuse me while I vomit in my mouth. I didn't think I could feel any worse... but the thought of having to scrape my way up to become *you*... that's horrible," she started crying again. "Just leave me alone."

Dickie's big back appeared in the cupboard door as he manoeuvred Casey and his chair clumsily into the Bridge. He barked at Ren to move some of the clutter out of his path and when she ignored him, he mumbled something about her time of the month. The Sub kept twisting against the reams of tape holding him to the seat being hoisted aloft by Dickie and Tom.

"I'm hurting," Casey said, his voice a plaintive whine. "It hurts. Stop. It isn't me."

"No! Don't keep him in here!" Ren stood up and wagged her finger frantically. "Not in here. Not him."

"Oh, do hush up, we have no choice, silly girl," Dickie said.

"No!" Ren ran at Dickie, pushing her hands into his back, stopping him from moving by wedging her feet against the floor. "Not him!"

"What the bloody hell are you doing, stupid girl?" Dickie said.

"I don't want him in here!"

"Mrs. Burns, try making yourself useful and get this ruddy child off me."

Sophie stepped forward and tried to coax her away, but she wouldn't yield. Dickie swung an elbow, knocking Ren's hands and making her stumble forward, her head brushing against the raised seat. Despite Casey being strapped tightly, his arms flat against his sides, he had enough purchase in his fingers to grasp a full fist of her hair. When she couldn't pull away, she screamed.

Dickie pulled the chair forwards, dragging Ren along with him. She reached a hand up and tried to pry open Casey's claw, but, like a spring trap, he snatched two of her fingers into his grip. The pressure made her hand pulsate, his squeeze as tight as a death spasm.

"I'm sorry, Ren," Casey shouted. "I want to stop. I don't want to do this."

Ren froze, her body helpless and her mind drifting to the safety of white noise.

"I'm going to bloody collapse," Dickie roared. "I need to drop the chair."

"No!" Sophie said, her legs jutting out of her tight skirt from seemingly impossible angles in an effort to stand underneath the chair and hold it up.

"What do you mean, 'no!'?" Dickie said.

"He won't let go of Ren. Don't drop him."

"Sod the sodding girl!" Dickie's beetrooting cheeks were vibrating, his eyes ready to ping from their doughy sockets. "I'm going to bloody well drop him!"

"Please don't," begged Casey. "I'm sorry, Ren. I don't want this. Oh, God. I don't feel good… make it stop!"

Sophie grabbed Ren's wrist and pulled, slipping her fingers from the Sub's vice grip. She managed to jerk Ren's hand away with a final tug. But, like a python coiling its prey, Casey's hand tightened on Ren's hair. The pain dragged her back into her body and she screamed again.

"It's the hair," Sophie said. "He won't let go of her hair!"

"STOP BEING BLOODY RIDICULOUS!" Dickie shouted. "It's only her ruddy hair. Pull it out, or chop it off. Do something."

"No," Ren said. "Not my hair. Please, Miss. Not my hair."

Sophie grabbed a pair of blue-handled scissors from the Bridge desk. "I'm sorry," she mouthed.

"No… please."

Dickie stamped on Sophie's foot, "Bloody well do it!"

Sophie opened the scissors and held them against the bunched roots below Casey's grip. The slow, snipping sound made Ren retch. The pressure on her scalp eased, then disappeared. Ren stepped back, quiet and dizzy, a wide patch of short, stinging bristles in the middle of her long, soft hair. She returned to her corner. Dickie and Tom dropped Casey's chair to the floor with a clatter.

"I'm sorry, Ren, it wasn't me," Casey said.

"Typical Sub," Dickie snapped, "blaming everyone else for your lack of control."

"I'm not... even a S... Sub," Casey said. "I'm in purgatory, it was only... another month before review. I was a... *Top*. I'm not supposed to be here," his slurred outrage sounded like the staccato bursts of a sleeping drunk. His head started shaking with exhaustion from all the swaying and biting. Tom reached out to grab his chin, anticipating a fit, but Casey immediately snapped at his fingers, only narrowly missing. "Don't. I can't help it... I can't stop."

"Casey," Dickie said, lowering his eyes to meet the boy's. "We are going to help you, that is all I have wanted, all along. We just underestimated how unhinged your type is, but we will save you."

"I'm not *their* type. I'm not... one of... one of them," Casey's head slumped as he wailed. "Ren, tell them, please... you're... one of my... friends, tell them what I am."

She turned away, her sob now a snuffle.

"It's no good asking her," Dickie said. "She's no use to anyone."

"Sh... she can tell you. The only reason I... demoted was because I didn't repent. There was nothing to... be sorry for... it was self-defence."

"It's sad to see a Sub so quickly revert to type, blaming others. Your weakness is disgusting."

"No… that's enough," Sophie ran her hands over the creases in her skirt, clearly uncomfortable with her cautious insubordination. "This isn't right, Dickie."

"You… sh… shut up," Casey said, turning to Sophie. "You're the… reason I got demoted. You blamed me for what happened when you knew it wasn't me. It was Dean… *as usual*. You knew what he did to me. You're just a stupid… bi-" Casey's pupils flickered up into his skull as he suffered another bout of frenzied biting.

"Calm, Casey. Calm down," Sophie hushed. "We're trying to help. We will help you. But you need to keep calm."

"I CAN'T!" he screamed, his nose and mouth dribbling a long trail from his bottom lip. "It's not me. I'm not… I'm not doing it!" His swollen, red eyes watered behind the Halo lens covered in clumps of sweaty fringe. "This is all you. It's your fault. It's whatever you… did to me downstairs. I shouldn't even be here. I'm a Sub because your Dean tried… beating me to death, while everyone laughed… and you just slapped his wrist."

"OK. OK… OK," Sophie said softly. "Just calm down. We don't know what's happening."

Dickie interrupted, again, "Whatever pickle you've got yourself into, we will sort it out. OK, young man?"

"NO!" Casey screamed. "I want… mum. Call my mum." He looked at Sophie and gurned with hate, "She always said you were a *bitch*. She… told me not to say sorry for bringing in a knife. You weren't doing anything. I wish… I *had* stabbed Dean. I wish I'd killed him."

Sophie stepped back, "... Let's just get on with it," she said.

Tom pulled the Block from his pocket. Casey shrieked and his eyes bulged. A wave of violent struggle rippled under the restraints, the tape stretched.

"Away! Put that away!" Casey stared at the Block and kept jolting his head forward. He snapped his teeth between words, "Do something. Get it away. It hurts." Tom quickly slid it under one of the blood-soaked cushions on the floor. But Casey continued, "It's no good… I know it's there… I need it… I can feel it. Someone stop it," Casey's eyes rolled to white again.

He stuck out his tongue and clamped his jaw down on it. He opened his mouth and blood poured from the deep punctures, then he lifted his head and spat into the air, a blast of red mist. Everyone jumped back, leaving Casey covered in his crimson froth. His eyes rolled back into view, terrified.

"You filthy beast," Dickie said, pale with disgust.

"Oh, God," said Sophie, softly shaking her head at the flap of tongue dangling from Casey Richardson's mouth. "This is bad. This is so very bad. What's wrong with them?"

"No!" Zach said. "By Jove, this is good. This is very good!" He strained to lift his head, the sudden realisation giving him a boost. "They went for me downstairs because they thought I had my Block. They've been after *me*, but it's the Block they want."

"Why is that good?" said Sophie.

"Deary me. Must I draw a picture? The hounds follow the fox! Someone needs to show the Subs the Block and make a run for it."

"Still not volunteering?" Tom asked Dickie. "… Thought not."

Tom pulled the Block from under the cushion and handed it to Zach. Casey's head lolled as he mouthed apologies, but his body bucked and strained. Zach stared at the clear glass and a bright glow lit up his hand as it unlocked. After a few presses, he'd disabled the screen lock.

"Done. When you get downstairs, turn on CTRL. The clients in range will appear on screen, coloured green. Select them all. Then, simply hit deactivate, twice. They turn red, then grey. Once they're grey, they can't be turned on again."

"And then what happens?" Tom said.

"Nothing. They'll just stop."

There was a long, deep bellow at the door. Brad had pressed his face up to the window and was staring at the Block. A cycle of different eyes carouselled, all of them fixing on the screen in Zach's hand. Then the eyes disappeared. There were a few seconds of silence, then a smash shook the room. The plaster around the door cracked in a continuous line around the whole frame. Another moment of silence. Another thud. Scatterings of wall fell onto the overturned bookcase. The crack widened. The Subs all stepped back in unison, ready for another charge.

"That door's not going to hold," Tom said.

"The other room. Now!" shouted Sophie. Ren didn't budge from her corner. "Now!" Sophie said again. She still didn't move. Her sobbing face was buried in her arm.

Tom shouted at the top of the girl's head, "*Ren, get up!*"

There was another thud. A large clump of plaster plummeted from above the door, exposing grey brick. Tom snatched the Block from Zach's hand, then grabbed Ren by the wrist and pulled her up.

Sophie grabbed Zach by his armpits and shouted at Dickie for help (who'd already made a run for the cupboard door). Dickie huffed before running back and grabbing Zach by the feet. They dragged his limp body, leaving Casey taped to his chair, screaming and gnashing. There was another thud, and a clatter, as bricks dropped loose. Tom dragged Ren into the adjoining room and tossed her wrist away in frustration.

"You're not the only one trapped, you know. Stop feeling sorry for yourself and grow up before you get someone else hurt. Please, Ren. Grow up."

Ren shook her head and ran for the hallway door before Tom could stop her. She stood in the corridor and froze, then dropped to her knees and tucked herself up against the stairwell doors. Tom ran out of the room to drag her back to safety, scooping her up like an infant. When he turned to take her back, a blur of Subs charged. Dickie was standing in the doorway.

"Run away," Dickie said. "Fix this," then he shut the door, leaving them in the corridor.

*   *   *

Tom carried Ren into the stairwell and cleared the first flight of stairs in two big jumps. He glanced over his shoulder and realised they hadn't been followed.

The Subs squeezed themselves around the looking glass of the adjoining room, they were allowing themselves another moment of calm, their bodies all swaying. And then, together, they beat their fists against the door, ten of them, hammering and screaming, and spitting, and scraping – snapping fingernails, tearing away skin. Like wild dogs, one would drop back and pace, then let out a howl before running back at the door, thumping into the wall. The rabid chorus would be interrupted by the desperate begging screams of apology as a Sub managed to separate their voice from their body, before being quietened by the shock of slamming against brick.

Tom gently lowered Ren's feet to the ground, whispering constant reassurance as he prised his arm away from her clutches.

"Ren, listen," for a moment, Tom forgot his anger and cupped her chin. "You run downstairs. See if you can get out the building, and wait there, OK? Don't come back in unless somebody fetches you. If you see any of *them*, just run home." He had to push her away before she gained the courage to carry on walking. She took a few steps, turned to stare at Tom once, then disappeared.

Tom held the Block above his head and shouted. The Subs turned, looked, paused, and leapt. Tom bolted down the stairs. He glanced behind. They weren't even running. They were jumping, *bounding* down the stairs, slapping their hands against the concrete floor before launching themselves.

Brad cleared an entire flight in a single leap, bouncing his shoulder off the wall. Ren was standing by the second-floor doors.

"*Why are you still here*?!" Tom screamed.

"I couldn't leave you," she reached out to him.

"*You stupid little girl!*"

Sally launched herself over the top handrail and clattered down the central gap onto the stairs in front of them. Her ankles crumpled as she landed. She was begging for everything to stop, but her hands kept dragging her broken body forward. Tom pulled Ren backwards and flung her through the doors to the second-floor corridor, screaming at her to run. She came to a sudden halt outside Tom's room. He managed to grab her by the collar and pull her head down just as Brad flung himself at them, jumping straight over them and skidding across the corridor. Tom stared into the camera box. The small pinhole stayed dark as he begged it to open. Brad started a new charge as it flashed green. He swung Ren into his room but a gaggle of arms clasped around his face when he tried to pull himself in. Tom clung to the door frame as fingers dug into his eyes. Ren grabbed him by his shirt and pulled him forward. He bent his head back, slipping through their grasps, and immediately turned and pushed his foot into the crush of Subs, all blocking each other from getting through the door. Above their matted heads, he saw Brad take two large steps backwards, point his head down and charge. They were all barged sideways, dragging Tom's foot with them. As his knee thumped into the door frame, the toppling weight snapped his leg towards the wall; he felt the crack through his entire body. Tom whipped his head back as a flash of agony floored him. He dragged his limp leg back into the room and Ren slammed the door shut. Snarling faces pressed against the window, and then, like upstairs, they started throwing themselves at the door.

Tom stared at the nauseating wet bulge pushing out from below his knee. Looking at his flopped foot made him dizzy, so he turned away.

"You stupid girl. You stupid, *stupid* girl..." he took a breath and blew out a surging sickness. "You stupid, selfish, little girl." Ren dropped to the floor and started to cry. "*Stop it*!" Tom blasted, making her jump with shock. "Stop your silly crying. You're the reason we're in this mess. You're the reason we're here. If not for your stupid lie, everything would be different. Take some responsibility. I will *not* die here today because of *you*. Stop crying. Take the Block, make a run for it. *You* need to fix this."

Ren sighed and stood up. Then she walked over to the cupboard and shut herself in. Tom dropped his head against the floor, stared at the ceiling, and listened to her muffled sob.

10

LAUREN TAMAR

Ren had spent the entire morning getting ready. Her appearance never used to be something that concerned her, not that she looked bad, or didn't care, but that she didn't care if *other people* thought she looked bad. Now she was constantly anxious, her outfit and make-up selection for the meeting had been decided and trialled days ago. She'd never been to the Bridge, but the letter stated it would be a chance to be completely honest, without judgement. She couldn't remember what it was like to sit in a room without needing to ignore *someone's* silent judgement.

That's what had broken her, the silence. She could rage against any fool who took her on, but she couldn't attack quiet glares. She became a collection of unspoken thoughts, dulled impulses. She used to have the strength to always say what needed to be said. She was effortlessly difficult. She could not be moved… until she was. Broken. Lost. Ren wanted to return.

Site had only demoted her to a mid. Her friends were talking to her again after months of being branded a 'slut.' And her mother had completely forgiven her. Her dad was still heartbreakingly disappointed, he hardly spoke to her, but her mum had said it would just take time.

She knew that Mr. Brown would be more understanding – he had to be. There were rumours that his wife had left him, that he'd locked himself in his house and had some kind of breakdown. But he was such a good man, he'd understand how sorry she was. She was desperate to finally tell him how much she regretted the lie, that it was all for attention, that she'd do anything to take it all back. She was certain he'd understand, if only a little, and show some forgiveness. She needed *his* forgiveness.

He was the best teacher she'd ever had – not like any of the others. And since Rego's takeover, things had become worse. Even though she was a Mid, a quarter of her lessons were now spent in one of the ground floor suites with hundreds of other clients, row after row of the dangerously stupid, all numbed by Halos. And whenever she was with a proper teacher, it wasn't the same, they only ever asked about work. If Mr. Brown was back, *if* he could forgive her, maybe she'd be allowed back into his lesson. Maybe she could start attending his revision sessions again. Maybe it could be like it was.

She walked into George's room and stroked his plump cheek until he woke. He beamed, a smile so gorgeous her chest ached at the thought it was for her.

"Morning, fat boy," Ren said in a deep growl. George laughed. He loved the growl. "I said morning, fatty," she growled again. He giggled so much he had to shove his face into his blanket to stifle his excitement.

He looked up and his brow suddenly furrowed, he was a picture of concentration, "Mornin'," he replied in the roughest squeak he could manage, forcing a cough that spluttered his laughter.

Ren picked him up, allowing her fingers to dig into his soft belly, making him squirm with delight. He wrapped his arms and legs around her tightly and she squeezed back as she carried him downstairs – the toddler's devotion reminding her she still had something.

Her dad was wearing one of his cartoon ties. He plucked George from her arms and placed him in the highchair, then lifted a spoon to his mouth before pulling it away as he was about to take a bite. George chuckled.

"Feed him properly," Ren's mum said, not needing to look up from what she was scrubbing in the sink.

Her dad made a mocking serious face. At fifteen, Ren thought she'd grown tired of her father's constant stupidity, that she was ready for a more mature relationship. But since her lie, now that he was only ever serious, she longed for silliness. He dropped the spoon in the bowl and yapped. The sudden noise caused Ren's mum to launch soapsuds into the air, and after the initial shock, George shrieked with laughter.

Ren sat down at the table and giggled, "So funny," she muttered.

Her dad didn't turn his head, he just kept fake feeding George with his back to his daughter. She was so fed up with embarrassment.

She passed up her dad's offer of a lift. He'd tried to insist, but, she'd already received her talking to the night before and didn't want to nod along to a repeat.

Yes, she was fully aware of the damage she'd caused. Yes, she was aware that it was a stupid, childish thing to do. Yes, she was aware that she did it all for attention. Yes, she was aware that the things she'd made up were not normal, healthy thoughts for a nice, fifteen-year-old girl, and even though she thought she was in love, she had no idea what that meant and she was just silly. She never used to let *anyone* patronise her, but the shame had been with her for so long it had soured.

After walking through the outskirts and heading for the main road past the first estate, she saw Dean turn the corner up ahead. He hadn't noticed her.

She wanted to shout for him but his name stuck in her throat while she decided on a tone – relaxed, playful, apologetic – what difference did it make if he was going to ignore her anyway?

A drink flew from the window of a passing car and splashed over him. She laughed, but, luckily, had stopped by the time he turned and saw her. Ren wanted to make a joke, it's what she would've done, and she would've managed to make him find it funny – but she'd been second-guessing for so long now, she greeted everything with timid indifference.

He smiled, only a glimpse of one, but she saw it. He ignored her when she tried to talk. She grabbed him when he tried to walk away, stopping him from making a stupid decision. He was breathing in that short, sharp way he always does before making one of his stupid decisions. She lied about needing to take the alley route to stop him from walking home. He kept a few strides ahead of her as they set off. Of all the bitter disregard, Dean's was the most painful. So many hypocrites had savoured the condemnation, teachers included, salivating at the chance to make their disgust known with a turn of the head or a sneer, but it *really* hurt when Dean had joined in.

They got to the alley entrance, an old church door propped up against the narrow gap between the pouch factory walls and a mile-long fence surrounding a Paradise Flats estate. Behind the door was a long concrete corridor with a jigsaw roof made of anything waterproof that could be lifted from the landfill. When the grotty tents poxing every spit of empty land had become too numerous to ignore, the Crusaders responded with predictable savagery. Hidden away areas like the alley became one of many havens for the homeless across the zones.

People lined the paving slabs, squeezed together, sharing torn sleeping bags, bundles of leaflets as mattresses. Ren and Dean tiptoed through the drunks, and the dirt, and the prayer circles, trying to ignore the unnerving desperation. Every step through the alley was heightened by unpredictability – the scrapings of the dregs, stripped of any semblance of dignity, displaying all emotions like exposed nerves. Any eye contact could initiate undying love, or blistering rage, or screeching hysteria. Everything was unfiltered. So, Ren and Dean kept their heads down until they got to the other side. And then they walked on, the spectacle as forgettable as it was grim. That was the way it had to be.

They stopped shy of the site fence. Ren saw a group of Subs in reception, Casey Richardson was one of them, so she ducked out of view as he turned. Dean carried on. She thanked him and said goodbye. If he'd heard her he, ignored it. She waited for them to clear before going inside, straight up to the Bridge.

She paced nervously. She'd planned to look at Mr. Brown, maybe smile, or make a muted apology straight away. But her gaze dropped to the floor when he appeared. He was skinnier and pale. His sad eyes had sunk into dark sockets. She hated seeing what she'd done. Mrs. Burns led them into the Bridge and pointed at the centre of the floor.

"Bag or chair?" she said.

"Pardon?" Ren whispered, panicking at the prospect of making a decision.

"Would you like to proceed with the meeting on chairs or beanbags? This is your forum."

"I'm not sitting on a beanbag," Mr. Brown said.

"Mr. Brown, as the adults here, we are to facilitate the wishes of the client."

"Chairs are fine," said Ren, managing to give Mr. Brown the smile she had been planning. He ignored it.

"Ok, we'll begin. Seven months ago, Lauren Tamar alleged that she and Mr. Tom Brown had been involved in a sexual relationship," Mrs. Burns said, her tone a scripted drone. "She stated that on two separate occasions they'd had intercourse on the premises of site 102. For the record, when the alleged incident took place, the site was not under the Rego family umbrella."

Ren buried her reddened face into her hands.

"This isn't necessary," Mr. Brown looked from side to side as if trying to find an escape route. "We all know what was said."

"...This bridge-building is being recorded to confirm closure," she pointed at a glass dome in the ceiling. "*Everything* in this room is recorded for the purposes of safeguarding. This environment is a sanctuary. I know this has been a particularly unpleasant experience for all involved. But, to adhere to the requirements of building this relationship bridge, we must first expose the foundations. *You cannot build on shaky ground,*" she said, pointing at the same mission statement written on the wall in swirling flowery letters. She continued, "One month into the investigation, Lauren altered her statement after footage was reviewed that disproved her original assertion. A further six weeks later, after numerous witnesses were interviewed, Lauren admitted that her story was a complete fabrication. As a consequence of the damage caused by the false claim, Mr. Tom Brown was unable to attend work due to ill health. He now feels ready to return. As Lauren sufficiently repented and had no previous sins, she was allowed to remain a Rego client. But, in order to move forward, I, Mrs. Burns, needed to facilitate the building of a bridge between Mr. Tom Brown and Lauren Tamar. Any questions?"

Ren peered out the top of her eyes and could see that Mr. Brown wasn't looking up. They both stayed silent.

"Good. Now, Lauren," Mrs. Burns said, "what happened?"

She took a deep breath and steadied herself. It was finally time to wipe the shame clean. "Mr. Brown was... *is*... my favourite teacher. I'd go to all his revision sessions. My dad says it was a stupid infatuation. I just wanted Mr. Brown to know I liked him. Some other kids started teasing me about him, calling me a 'suck.'" Ren was conscious of how wobbly her voice was, but she persisted, "I was embarrassed, like they thought I was a child. I just wanted to show them. So, I said we... you know... so I said we did it. It wasn't supposed to turn into this."

"Mr. Brown, do you acknowledge?" said Mrs. Burns. He nodded. "Thank you for your understanding. Lauren, thank you for your honesty. Next question. What were you thinking then, and now?"

"Then? I don't know," said Ren. "... Lonely... and silly, like a kid. Now I'm ashamed. And sad... I'm so sad. I want to turn things back, I long for it. Sometimes I get lost in a fantasy where it's all before I ruined it and I would give everything for that, but it can't be undone and I feel broken by how sad I have made everything."

"Mr. Brown, do you acknowledge?" said Mrs. Burns, continuing with her script. He nodded. "Thank you for your understanding. Lauren, thank you for your honesty. Next question. Who has been affected?"

Suddenly, Mr. Brown started sobbing. First, a whine, then his face scrunched, and his breathing shuddered. And he let go – a big, whimpering cry.

Ren's cheeks flushed, her voice cracked, "Everyone. My parents hate me, my friends hate me. My dad thinks I'm a *slut*, but I deserve it... Mr. Brown has been affected the most. I've ruined his life... I guess... I don't know," she started blubbing, "I know it caused problems. I'm sorry. I'll say it a million times. I'm sorry."

"Mr. Brown, do you acknowledge?" said Mrs. Burns. He nodded. "Thank you for your understanding. Lauren, thank you for your honesty. Final question before Mr. Brown will respond. Lauren, what needs to be put right?"

"All of it. And I don't know how," Ren cried. "I just want to go back. I've said sorry. I am sorry. It will never happen again, I swear. I just want it like before. Mr. Brown, you were the best teacher ever, I just want to be back in your lessons. I just want to forget everything."

Ren gave in to her despair and wailed like an abandoned infant, so helplessly loud any stray parent would come running. Between the tiny moments of silence, as she sucked in for her next bawl, Ren could hear that Mr. Brown was as bad, batting their misery back and forth in a rally of hysteria.

"Whenever you're both quite ready," Mrs. Burns said, waiting. She tapped her foot, sucked at her teeth, stared at each of the colourful posters stuck on the walls. They were still crying so she handed them several tissues from a box covered with smiley face stickers and repeated herself. Mr. Brown brought his episode to an end with a deep, throat clearing, sigh. "Mr. Brown, do you acknowledge?" said Mrs. Burns. He sucked in a wet sniffle and nodded. "Thank you for your understanding. Lauren, thank you for your honesty. Mr. Brown, it is your turn to repair your side of the bridge, please, expose the foundations."

Spreading pinpricks of relief travelled up Ren's neck and into her head, tickling her scalp. She had finally told him how sorry she was. By openly accepting all the blame that everyone had been heaping on her for so long, for the first time she felt free from its weight. She wiped her sticky face and smiled at Mr. Brown, a genuine smile, not the plastered twitch she used to stop her mum from telling her to cheer up. Mr. Brown didn't smile back.

He swallowed, "I also want to forget everything... but I can't. I never will. My wife *left* me." Mr. Brown finally looked at Ren, but all she saw was hate. "Lauren, she *left* me," he gulped, "I feel sick, *physically* sick, at the thought of teaching again. I'm... drowning... and *you* want to be put back in *my* classroom? Are you *that* selfish? Are you *that* stupid?"

"Mr. Brown. Bridges aren't built with judgement," Mrs. Burns said firmly.

He nodded an apology. "Lauren, there is no way you will *ever* step foot in my classroom again. The only reason you have stayed in 102 is because I agreed to it. After all, I know you made a mistake. An awful, hideous mistake, but still just a mistake. But I will *never* talk to you again. I will *never* teach you again," he lowered his head and returned to weeping. "I never want to look at you again," he whispered.

The words didn't register with her immediately, just a small stir of the coming despair, a swirl of unrest ready to surge when Ren was capable of accepting what he'd said.

"Lauren, do you acknowledge?" said Mrs. Burns. She gave a slight nod, "Thank you for your understanding. Mr. Brown, thank you for your honesty. I will devise a contract for all parties to sign, but I agree that contact between the two of you will be kept to an absolute minimum. Lauren, I think you should be grateful that this is the extent of your punishment. Thank you both for allowing this bridge to be built. In time may it be a sturdy monument to the restorative practice championed by Rego." Mrs. Burns looked at the dome in the ceiling and nodded to signal the end of the meeting.

Ren responded dizzily to the request to stand. She felt weightless as she followed the adults into the corridor. Her dad had spat out his judgement when he said it was a silly infatuation, a stupid child's embarrassing fantasy. But what she was feeling wasn't childish. When she finally understood that Mr. Brown hated her, when she felt that thump, and she stared at the poison in his face, it was the most painful thing she'd ever experienced. Heartbreak is such a weak description because the hurt was everywhere, overwhelming and constant. She loved him so much – she only ever wanted him to see her as something more – and now that would never be. She was hollow, and at the same time, stuffed with sadness, bloated and cold, and there was nothing she could do.

Her ears blocked and her vision blurred as her thoughts pulled her focus into the distance. This felt like a despair that could never be escaped. If she were stood at the top of the stairwell, she would have thrown herself down, or leaned over and let herself drop. She could step into traffic on the way home. Or hide under her quilt and silence her mum's hopeful lies with a fistful of tablets. Or she could use her dressing gown cord, and let her dad walk in on her swollen, purple face – see if he still found her so disappointing when he was trying to tear the knot from her distended neck. Ren knew she was going to do it – she didn't know how, but she *was* going to do it. There was no way back for any part of her that she still liked. She only knew that she wanted to cuddle her brother once more, and then she would do it. Facedown in the bath would be warm and quiet.

There were screams and shouts. She looked up at the panic and confusion. A man, covered in blood, dropped into Mr. Brown's arms, and before she knew it, she was bundled back into the Bridge.

The sight of the walls and the smell of the air made her feel sick. The chairs were still in the arrangement from the meeting she'd suffered through. The bloodied man lay on the floor, red pooling around a gaping wound in his back. The door thudded. Ren had no idea what was happening. She didn't care.

"We're trapped in here?" said Mr. Brown.

He glanced at Ren, but his eyes were blank. He wasn't even thinking about the meeting anymore, or her. He didn't care. Ren tucked herself into a corner and began to cry. She just wanted to be home, with her dad, being silly, and George, laughing. But that was lost.

11

"FOR HIS OWN GOOD"

Zach's eyelids were getting heavy again. A foggy headache was thumping away any thought he held for more than a few seconds.

Sophie gently tapped his face, "Zach, stay awake." She turned to Dickie, "What shall I do?"

"How on Earth should I know? You fancied yourself as a medical expert. This is your site. You work it out. But keep slapping him. If he pops his clogs, it will make this whole farce far more complicated for you. Do whatever you need to do."

"Zach!" she shook his face. "Talk to me. Say something, stay here," his eyes rolled and he looked up. "Tell me about yourself. Tell me anything."

He licked his dry lips and shuffled his head up her lap, some life returned.

"Like what?" he croaked.

"How long have you been at Rego?" Sophie said, clutching at the first thing on her mind. The only thing that was always on her mind.

"That's your idea of how to help?" Dickie said. "Having a gossip. Would you like some biscuits for your knitting circle?"

"How long?" Sophie repeated, ignoring Dickie's sneer.

"Years. But I'm new to Ed. I was in Medical, and Mr. Drexler had an idea about something I'd been toiling on," Zach was calm now, almost serene, his eyes closed as if he were whispering in his sleep. "There was something about the chance to work in education, to help right some wrongs. It was Dr.Vaneman... Dickie... Sir, who inspired me." He coughed feebly and winced. "You were announcing a site takeover on a Broadcast. You spoke with such passion and sincerity about changing the fortunes of those clients... discipline and integrity... you kept repeating those words."

"Yes! Yes!" Dickie nodded. A huge smile for a fond memory, clearly delighted that the conversation had centred on him. "I remember. Great speech. Discipline and integrity... great speech."

"It spoke to me, how the only difference between success and failure is effort. It's what my father always used to tell me... *ignavum fortuna repugnant.*"

"Yes," Dickie said, still nodding, "... Ign... um... fortune pugnut... exactly. I've dedicated my life to trying to teach that lesson. We need to make sure we never forget all the good we do. It's the reason I get up in the morning."

Dickie gave Zach a heavy pat of encouragement. Zach ignored the pain it caused.

"Subs need guidance," Zach said. "They are their own worst enemy. Learning is key and with the right get up and go attitude, they can work themselves out of their slump. It's the final piece of the jigsaw in making this Nation truly great. And I thought I'd solved it, found a way to help teach these Subs. It was supposed to make them behave. Discipline and integrity."

"This is just a hiccup, man, have faith," Dickie said, his nod so constant that it looked like he was being electrocuted. "Do you think I got everything right the first time? Well… actually, yes, I did… but still, it takes perseverance. A man must be resilient. I'm sure, thanks to your work, future Rego sites will have near zero percent delabelling."

"But!" Sophie barked, a sharp interruption followed by a slow breath. "… But, don't we want more than that?"

Dickie's nodding shook to a halt and he smirked, a mini smile of pity for the little lady, "What more could we want, my itsy-bitsy birdie?" he said with a sing-song tone, leaning in to tickle her chin with a gnawed nail.

"Everything we do is worthless! *By choice*! Zero percent, ten, fifty, delabelling – it's all noise. The data says what we want. Something is always fudged. Everything is meaningless. And we convince idiots it's for their own good. We don't want them out of their slump, we want them to live in it, gratefully. It's wrong, we should be teaching them *how* to think, not what to think."

"Teach these things *how* to think!" Dickie laughed.

Zach ignored a hot ripple of nausea to join in. He adored healthy debate, always willing to pounce into any conversation in need of a devil's advocate. "*How* to think," he repeated, laughing again. But that was all he had the energy for. A deep sadness swilled in with the nausea. He was relieved to hear Dickie continue.

"You've changed your tune since your interview. You're not so impressive when you get your little brain doing more than fluttering your lashes. If you teach these things how to think, they'll only learn how to disagree. You've seen the protests, haven't you? They are a scourge. Anti-nationalists with fancy ideas are killing this Nation. What these … *things* need is more of their time occupied, and *less* thinking for themselves until they prove they can think properly. They *should* be grateful. They've earned none of what they're given, and they still complain about how bad it is. Things aren't *that* bad."

"For you!" she said.

"Or you!" Dickie replied. "I don't see you turning your nose up to everything I provide. You're on the wrong side, Mrs. Burns. You know what *they're* capable of; today's naughties are tomorrow's criminals. You've seen the leaflets."

"The propaganda pamphlets, yeh, I've seen 'em," Sophie said with a hint of her hidden accent. Dickie turned away. "Last month my husband was fitting locks to the bins because of 'Vegetable Scrap Thieves.' Men'll believe all sorts of folly to ignore their impotence!"

"It's not just vegetables," Zach said, sensing that Dickie was losing interest. "I know their type, they only want ruin.

CTRL will change that. The atrocities are almost weekly, and it's getting worse – the Broadcast said they tried to bomb a church yesterday... *a church*! They interviewed one of the congregation, an innocent child... lucky to be alive. Anyone who'd do that to a child is a monster."

"It terrifies me," Sophie said, "how stupid intelligent people choose to be."

"It's true!" Zach lifted his head an inch, mustering as much passion as his feeble body would allow. "It terrifies *me* how shrill women think everything's a conspiracy. Why would the Nation lie? Subs want to destroy us. *Veritas*. But, there is hope, their actions are a symptom of ignorance. If one works, one succeeds. Circumstances are an excuse. I didn't have it easy, my father had me working weekends to help cover my education. If Subs could only be taught, they'd understand the way to success is through work. Dissent achieves nothing." Zach held a wide grin. Stab wound or not, he couldn't let a female's feelings get in the way of facts. Then he vomited again, in the same spot on Sophie's lap, before passing out, coddled by a surge of deep satisfaction.

*   *   *

Sophie stopped stroking Zach's head and used the back of her hand to push the frothy puke off her lap and onto the floor. She wanted to poke a finger into his shoulder hole.

She had surpassed peak disgust long ago. Her existence was an exercise in endurance. Her defence was a cold, condescending calm. But these were the conversations that knotted her insides, creating the ulcers that would burn to stomach cancer – flatulent anecdotes that fuelled unbending opinions which shaped overarching decisions. And what (with all her experience, and spirit, and obstinate insistence that, deep down, she was truly principled) did she ever do about it? Nothing.

She felt the remnants of her husband's morning imposition trickle out. She wanted to shower.

"Oh, for goodness sake," Dickie shouted, slamming the cupboard door. "Why are they taking so long? Why are you all so ruddy useless?" The shock jolted Zach.

"Shhhh," Sophie hissed.

"Oh, shush yourself. Apologies for being concerned with keeping Zach alive," Dickie said. "Where are those two? They should have turned off those bloody animals by now. Something must be done, otherwise, Zach's a goner for sure."

"Don't say that. What can we do?"

"... The boy!" Dickie pointed to the hole in the cupboard wall leading through to the room Casey was in. "We need to let him go."

"What? Why? How will that help Zach?"

"Because, if anyone arrives and sees that *thing* tied up here, near us, Zach will be the least of our worries. Any more silly questions?"

"I think our time would be better spent on other things, rather than trying to cover our backsides."

"When I want to hear what *you* think, I'll make sure to tell you in advance what to say. Don't forget who you're talking to, little lady. Let's remember, you are responsible for this site, and frankly, it's in turmoil." Sophie looked at Dickie with a revulsion usually saved for the back of her husband's snoring head. "Now get up…" he said. She sat still. "That's an order! … Now!" she gently slid Zach off her lap and stood up, her eyes burning into her boss, not that he showed the merest hint of concern.

"Fine," she said.

Dickie smiled, "There's a good girl."

Sophie *longed* for her shower.

They walked through to the bridge. Casey was weeping and whispering to himself, praying for it all to stop, then his head slumped. Dickie walked across the room and kicked clumps of brick and plaster away and heaved the toppled bookcase to one side. The door scraped the floor as he opened it, hanging uneven in its broken frame. Casey tried to bite stray hands as they pushed his chair through the yellow puddle that trickled around his feet, shoving him out into the hallway. With Casey's back to the Bridge, Dickie handed Sophie a pair of plastic scissors. She reached her arm through the doorway and dragged them down the reams of tape wrapped around the back of the chair. A few strands cut loose. She slashed at it again. Casey was still stuck tight. She pressed one end of the scissors down the back of the tape from the top and tried snipping, but their blunt chew just bunched the strands together. She closed the scissors and pulled at the strands, her fingers turned white before she finally managed to snap through. Casey squirmed with the loosening of his restraints, the extension cord just enough to stop him from breaking free. There was no way she could cut through those wires.

"Now what?" Sophie said.

"Untie him," Dickie replied.

"I can't untie him, I'd need to get too close. We just need to leave him up here."

"No! Absolutely not. The last thing you want is for anyone to see that you stood idly by while Tom tied one of these monsters up. Besides, maybe he's made himself useful. Maybe he's about to turn those mongrels off. We must let the boy go, for his own good, he needs to be with the others."

"Fine," Sophie snapped. "Fine. Whatever you say. You need to hold him then if I'm going to untie."

After a brief pause, Dickie suddenly scurried over to the window ledge. He picked up the broken belt Tom had discarded, then walked out into the corridor and looped the leather over Casey's head, allowing it to drop below his chin. Casey's jaw stopped snapping and his eyes rolled back into view as he struggled for lucidity.

"What... what'sh happening?" he slurred, his fat tongue flapping in the way of his mouth.

Sophie shook her head and hushed in his ear.

"What'sh... on my neck? What are you... what are you going to do?" his pleading was almost incoherent, like a dementia patient begging strangers in a ward. "Are you going to...? Pleash don't. I'm shhorry, OK, I'm shhorry. You're right, I'll take reshponshibility, whatever it ish, whatever I've done. I'll do anything you need me to do. I'm shhorry. Don't hurt me. Pleash... Msh Burnsh, look at me..." Sophie shook her head and turned away. "Msh Burnss, pleash, you were right. I shouldn't have brought the knife in. I should've apologish. My Mum wash wrong, you're not a bishh. I know you're only trying to help. I promish I'll be better. I'll be whatever you tell me to be. Pleash don't kill me."

"We're not going to kill you, ridiculous boy, we're helping you. This is for your own good. Help is coming," Dickie said, then he yanked the belt tight.

Casey's head jolted backwards as he tried to squeeze his pleading through the choking strap. His body went rigid with fight, trying to break out of the cable holding him to the chair.

"That's too hard. You'll hurt him!" shouted Sophie.

"Then you best get a ruddy move on," Dickie said.

Sophie ran around to face the boy. She ripped the tape still wrapped around his legs and he instantly started kicking. She shoved her body against his feet and grimaced as he dug his heels into the top of her thighs. Casey stretched out his fingers, trying to pull his arms up to scratch at her. Dickie gripped his leash as he saw Sophie pull at the plug weaved through the loops of cable to hold it tight.

"Are you ready?" she asked.

Dickie tugged his belt and nodded, a fit of coughs burst from Casey's veined throat.

Sophie pulled the cable until there was a hole large enough to squeeze the plug free, it flopped down and the cord around Casey's stomach slackened. He shot his hands up and grasped at Sophie's hair, but she pulled away just as Dickie yanked back. Casey turned his attention to the leash holder, stumbling off his chair and leaping at him, but Dickie swiftly pulled the belt down, clattering Casey to the floor. Dickie plumped his big knees into the pleading boy's back.

"We'll need to drag him like this," said Dickie, "then let him free when we get downstairs."

Sophie nodded weakly, not wasting time pretending there was a line she wouldn't cross. She grasped the Sub by the ankles, holding them against the floor. Dickie counted to three, then pulled on the belt as Sophie lifted his feet, pushing him like a broken wheelbarrow. They dragged him a body length down the corridor, with an eruption of spluttering. Sophie blocked out the noise. They pulled him to the stairwell in a series of choking drags. The child howled with each painful bump down the two flights of stairs; every time he tried to stand and attack, Sophie grabbed his feet and Dickie pulled the leash, stretching out his body and keeping him pinned to the floor gulping for breath, squealing like a piglet to slaughter.

They saw the Subs on the second-floor corridor, throwing themselves against a wall.

"I'm assuming those imbeciles have locked themselves in that room. That was *not* part of the plan... ruddy useless," Dickie said.

"We need to help them."

"We do *not*. There is nothing we can do to help. They will be fine. Look, a team will be here shortly to sort this mess. We need to let *this* Sub go, and get back upstairs. Today has been a ruddy disaster." Dickie released the belt and quickly stepped back. "Let him go."

Casey shrieked and scrabbled away, running straight past the doors to the second-floor corridor and down the stairwell.

Sophie looked at Dickie, "He was *supposed* to join the others," she said.

"Oh, do stop your whining, woman. What sodding difference could it possibly make?" He turned and trudged back up to the top floor, his hands planted into the meat of his thighs as he laboured to drag his hefty frame.

Sophie watched him waddle, listening to the scrape of his shiny trousers as they disappeared into the folds at the top of his triangle legs. No matter her daily strain – the feet-throbbing, head-splitting, back-breaking, thankless slog – she knew her view would never improve. Dickie's large arse shuffled around the corner. Sophie followed it.

*   *   *

"Ren?" Tom said. "Ren, you need to come out. Ren?" The rhythmic thump against the door continued. Plaster sprinkled the floor. They didn't have long. "*REN*?!"

"Why do you hate me?" she said from the cupboard.

"I... I don't hate you...OK?" Tom said, his frustration simmering. "Look, this isn't important at the moment. *God, why are you so selfish*!?" Her crying escalated. "... I don't hate you. Please, come out." There was a splintering crack. Tom darted his eyes at the door, then dragged himself over and slumped against it. The thuds continued, but Tom's weight dampened them. "Ren, *please.*"

The cupboard door opened slightly.

"Why do you hate me?" she whispered.

"I don't... I get it, OK. I understand how it happened," Tom's voice had a soft sincerity that pulled her forward. "I don't even blame you. But I nearly lost my job. You can't just expect me to move on from something like that."

"I'm sorry. I keep saying it. I'm sorry. I just wanted to be back in your lessons. When I heard you were coming back, I thought, I hoped, I hoped *so* much, that it could be like before."

Tom slid Zach's Block from his back pocket but kept it on the floor behind him, out of view of the Subs.

"Get out of here, with the Block, and I'll talk to Mrs. Burns, I promise. We'll come to some kind of arrangement. But right now, the only thing that is important is that we get *them* switched off. Ren, you are the only one that can do it."

The door rattled and brick dust and plaster showered Tom's hair.

"But... I don't know what to do... I'm just… a silly..."

"I'll shuffle to the corner, you let them in, they'll come for me. You show them the Block and make a run for it. You'll have a head start. You just need to get to the ground floor before they get you. Then switch them off."

"I'll not make it."

"You *will*, Ren. Now isn't the time for crying. You've been doing that all morning. You need to stop being afraid. You *need* to grow up."

"That's why you think I've been crying? Because I'm afraid? I'm not scared of them. I don't care what they do to me, as long as it's quick. I've been crying because of *you*! Nothing will hurt me the way you did when you said we'll never see each other again. That's worse than anything those things can do. I know I'm just a silly girl. I know I lied about us having sex. I know everyone thinks I'm stupid and embarrassing. I'm sorry. I can't help it. I can't do it."

"You can."

"*I can't do it!*"

"... I'm sorry..." Tom said, he rubbed his palms into his eyes, trying to loosen the words from his throat. "... You can do this, Ren. I know you can do this because *you* are strong. Because... because the person I fell in love with was strong. I love you, Ren."

Ren looked up. She didn't want to give in to the elation, maybe she'd misunderstood, maybe he didn't mean it.

"Do you mean it?" she asked.

"I did nearly lose my job because of you. But you had nothing to do with my wife. Whatever we had was already gone, that wasn't your fault. I never knew I wanted to end it with her. Until you came along. Such a beautiful, inquisitive, young thing. You reminded me what it was like to have someone laugh with me again. I mean *really* laugh. You reminded me what it was like to want someone again."

"But I lied about you... I ruined what we had," the fifteen-year-old said. "I told people we'd... you know. I thought I'd lost you."

"You haven't lost me. I know why you did it," he said, his eyes warm, looking at her the way she'd wanted since first being invited back into the Bridge. It was a well-practised look, perfected on countless girls whose flickering lashes had offered a new distraction from his monotony. So many pretty young things he'd made giggle over the years. But it took someone as special as Ren to persuade him to take a more persistent approach. She had been the first where he'd let it become something more. "After that Christmas revision session, the first time I kissed you, do you remember?" she nodded with the brightest smile. "You taught me to love again... you saved me. You're not a stupid, little girl. You're an enchanting woman. I know I once promised we'd be together and I still want that, more than anything." The door thudded, more plaster dropped. Ren started crying again. But, for the first time in so long, because she was happy. She let herself fill with the peace that thousands of longing fantasies never brought. "I know why you lied," Tom said, grasping both her hands in his. "And, in time, I *will* forgive you for that. For us to have anything there can be no lies. Do you understand? But what you lied about, don't think I don't want it. I want it so much I ache. I just wanted to treat you with the respect you deserve. But, Ren, unless we get out of here, *they* will break through that door, and we'll never get our chance."

After the months of rejection, the insults, and the stinging disappointment, it all drifted away. All those that dismissed her were wrong. None of them mattered. She had everything she wanted.

"I love you, Mr. Brown." She leaned forward, resting her head on his chest, then she reached behind his back and slid the Block into her sleeve.

Tom gave her a long, hard kiss on the forehead before pushing her away, "Remember," he said. "Wait for them all to run in, but then show them you have it as soon as possible."

Tom dragged himself to the corner of the room opposite the door. Ren pinned herself against the wall and held the handle, ready to open it against herself.

Tom picked up the empty backpack he'd left on a chair that morning and held it up as a shield. Ren pulled the handle on the door. It crashed open, smashing into the wall, squeezing her into the corner behind it. The Subs sprinted straight at Tom, flinging themselves across the room. He folded his body over his limp leg as they descended, a flurry of blows pounded his back. One grasped at his loose ankle and he beat it away with his rucksack. Ren screamed and held up the Block. The realisation rippled through the Subs and, in turn, they stopped flailing. Their bodies convulsed with desire. Ren ran. They roared, and growled, and spat, and shrieked. And then they followed.

Tom was alone. The sickening pain below his knee returned with the silence. He tried to mask the throb with thoughts of that first kiss, catching Ren off-guard by getting her to lean in with whispered revision instructions, watching the shock in her expression soften to acceptance, then desire, as he held her head in place for a second attempt. But the agony didn't soften, because the memory had been soured by the silly girl who wasn't mature enough to keep their secret.

"I don't want to do this," said a weak voice, "but I'm not sorry it's you."

Tom looked over to where the voice had come from. Sally Simon looked at him, two sad pinpricks of life glistening in the centre of her bashed eyes – so swollen they had closed into thin slits in her bloody face. She slowly pulled herself towards him.

"Sally, no! What are you doing? Listen to me, Sally, you can control this, you need to control yourself."

Tom started toppling desks to block her path.

"I can't stop it. It's not me," she cried. "But you deserve it."

"No, Sally. Listen. *Listen*. I'm begging you," Tom cycled through an array of tones, trying to say something in a way that would stop her crawling forwards. "*Listen*. You stupid fucking girl. Control yourself. Please. FUCKING LISTEN!"

She used his loose ankle to pull herself onto him. Tom yelled and his head span, nearly passing out with the pain. By the time his vision stopped reeling, her hands were clamped into his chest. She pressed her mouth onto his stomach and it filled with the soft bit of stubborn tummy not lost to his months of depressed starvation. She released a long breath through her nose, contemplating what she knew she was about to do, preparing herself for the taste. Then she bit down hard.

12

DICKIE VANEMAN

Dickie woke to the soft chirps of happy birds and the warm, pure light of morning sun shining around the edges of his glossy bedroom walls. He was annoyed. He wanted the gentle wave sound with a tropical sea glow. Having been so vexed by his incorrect wake routine, he'd insisted on snoozing his alarm repeatedly for over an hour. The additional bouts of much-deserved sleep did little to stem his displeasure. He'd asked his Janet to alter the settings days ago and hated that he'd need to repeat himself. He could hear her in the kitchen, clattering pans and fussing with drawers.

He spoke into the screen above his head, "My Janet, I'll take my breakfast in bed this morning. That is all."

"… …" Dickie could hear her breathing through the receiver. "… I'm so sorry, Dr. Vaneman, Sir. I'm trying to catch up, I really am, but I'm running behind. My mum had a bad night…"

"Janet, no babbling. Is my breakfast ready? A simple yes or no."

"... No, Sir."

Dickie kicked his thick duvet off his body and marched out of his room. She didn't deserve the courtesy of him finding his dressing robe. If she couldn't even cook his ruddy eggs in the morning, he would walk around his own bloody house as naked as the good Lord intended.

"I'll take a fresh juice. Immediately, Janet." He plumped his backside on his breakfast bar stool.

She quickly dropped his favourite fruits into the juicer, then placed a filled glass on the resin counter. Dickie grabbed her hand before she could scuttle away. His tummy was shielding her from the sight of the shrivelled, moist tip poking out below, but she still kept her eyes firmly to the side.

"I like you, very much," Dickie breathed. "You've been... very... fulfilling. But you are slipping of late. I suggest you try harder because I would like for us to stay friends."

"Yes, Sir. Sorry."

"Would you like to stay friends?" he tickled her nose with his fingertip.

"Yes, Sir."

"Lovely. I'm pleased we had this chat," he said, still squeezing her slender fingers in his grip. "All is forgiven if you give me that winning smile. Come on, let me see." Dickie raised her chin with his finger and waited for her smile to be broken by the cheeky tip of a stuck-out tongue, the way he'd taught her, the way he liked it. When she obliged, he wrapped a thick arm around her back and opened his legs to pull her in. "My brazen little birdie," he said, laughing, like a father secretly enjoying his child's naughtiness. His voice danced like a lullaby, "Now, why will I forgive you?"

"Because you're a soft daddy bear," she whispered.

"Whose soft daddy bear?"

"Mine," she said, too quietly.

Although the movement was so slight as to appear almost non-existent, her face turned away from his. She wasn't doing her bit properly and Dickie was losing patience. Keeping an arm pressed into her back, he reached under her apron with his free hand and held his clenched fist against her backside.

"And who's being a cheeky birdie?" he sang.

"Me," she said.

Dickie raised his thumb and pushed it up until it felt the warmth in between the crack of her bottom. He looked at her expressionless face, barely managing to make her gasp with each hard shove of his thumb, prompting her to do her bit. Finally, she giggled for him and cracked her half-smile with the tip of her tongue, but it was pointless. No ruddy effort whatsoever. Even if he touched himself, he'd barely dribble onto her feet, not worth the bother, he thought, shoving her away and swallowing his juice in one dripping gulp.

"You're ugly today," he said.

Dickie slid off his stool and squeezed past her as she scurried over to wipe the buttock-shaped, furry silhouette of sweat off the leather seat.

After opting for his cardinal plum suit, he took a stroll through the village plaza to help him de-stress after the morning's frustrations. It was a warm day, the delivery drones were buzzing through the blue skies. A few laps of the White Oak would calm him. It was his favourite bit of the centre. Like all the trees in the village, it was plastic, only much, much larger. Its shiny canopy branched overhead, pulsing a colourful glow as it purified the creeping smog from the faraway zones. The bunting was out and a brass band was playing in the cobble market. He wandered through to collect a coffee and mini-pastry assortment from a quirky street barista, resplendent in Victorian-era clothing with a fine moustache, then strolled home via the duck pond. He got into his car, put it into auto-drive, reclined his seat, and watched the white branches glide by, then dialled Mr. Drexler.

"Good morning. I didn't wake you, did I?" Dickie said. "*I've* been up for hours, already got a brisk gym session under my belt."

"Funny," Mr. Drexler said. "I thought you spent your mornings lying in bed and stuffing your face with pastries."

Dickie laughed, a nervous noise to try and hide his annoyance at the incisive barb, a noise he frequently made when talking to Mr. Drexler.

"We trial today, in case you'd forgotten," Dickie said, his voice deeper, trying to grapple back some authority. "The broadcasters are in at three, ready for airing at five. Once again, well done on all the string-pulling. I think today is the day Rego cements its legacy," Dickie gave a hearty laugh.

"What can I help you with?" Mr. Drexler said, his voice flat.

"Remember, I need a lab monkey. I know I'm good, but a hand is always appreciated," he laughed again.

"Zachary Noblie-Goggins is on site."

"Who's that?" Dickie asked.

"Someone who knows what they're doing?"

"You are my rock, Mr. Drexler, the glue that holds me together. I couldn't do this without you. Oh, one other thing, do we have any spare Janets? Mine is useless."

"I have no idea," Mr. Drexler said, before hanging up.

Dickie pulled a face, furious at the bruising exchange. He'd never liked Mr. Drexler. The man had no warmth, and his exotic muddle of accents made him sound so aloof. Dickie was counting the days until he could be a little more frank with him, educate him on his bedside manner. Dickie loved the gamesmanship; the scheming, the plotting, the position-ing – it's what he was good at - greasing the right palms and trickling a little oil in the right ears. Dickie looked forward to the day he could manoeuvre himself above Mr. Drexler, he'd take great pleasure in ruining a man so convinced of his superiority.

Lost in a warm fantasy of boardroom espionage, it took the invading stench of the nearby landfill for Dickie to realise he'd entered the zone. The auto-drive was not designed for their potholed excuse for roads. The front tyre clunked over a crevice, causing Dickie to accidentally squeeze his cappuccino, popping the lid off. He tilted the cup and shouted at his dashboard to lower the window, casting his drink outside before it could gush onto his leather interior or purple jacket.

Dickie had given up on ever being surprised at what he witnessed in the zone. Not an inch wasn't daubed with filthy graffiti – the pithy messages of pissy snowflakes who'd never learned to catalogue their concerns legitimately. And everyone was so skinny – no meat to their miserable bones. There was no excuse, meal pouches provided more calories than their little imaginations should know what to do with. It was because they never slept, Dickie thought, up all night vandalising and doing God knows what to each other. There always seemed to be so many of them wandering around aimlessly. Between the Lines, and the bus loads of Joes and Janes, the unoccupied rate was supposed to be less than one percent. But a glance at the hordes of bare-footed mothers, prowling the pavements in their grubby nightgowns, proved that wasn't the case. CTRL was going to be a real game-changer. He'd only skim read the document about his new initiative, but the data had convinced him it was the next step in shooting for the moon.

Dickie pulled up to his parking space only to find it filled with some drab green monstrosity. He stifled a deluge of expletives by changing each curse to gibberish at the last moment, then he snatched a piece of paper from his briefcase and scribbled a furious note –

'To the owner of the cheap green car,

This space belongs to Dr.Richard Vaneman. CEO of Rego Education. If you were in any doubt, there is a large sign which indicates this to be the case. Unless of course, you cannot read, which would come as no surprise, given your inability to afford a vehicle befitting a person of real worth.

You are a disgrace. Your filthy manners are an alarming sign that our society still has a long journey ahead before reaching its goal of acceptable civility worthy of His image. If you ever park in my space again, I shall personally see to it that your laughably sub-standard automobile is recycled, and you are appropriately punished.

Stern regards,

Dr.Dickie, Esq. CEO, BBS, MBS, FUNV.'

He placed the folded note under the wiper and mumbled a final 'fuc...rubbertrub bastar...raster coc...aninnie cun...nchy nut,' while toe-poking the tyre with the tip of his patent leather shoes.

Dickie walked into the site and, as was customary, had a quick roam of *his* building, to make sure all was tip top. He spotted Sophie on the top floor and crept up from behind to surprise her with a playful poke. Dickie understood the importance of occasional light-hearted japery, plus he wanted to make sure she wasn't secretly saying anything untoward.

"Piling on the timber, chunky," he whispered to her, pinching her hip. "It's disappointing to see you let such a fine figure spoil. Am I not working you hard enough?"

She introduced him to Mr. Brown, and his first impression was exactly as expected from the paperwork. Dickie was wholly unimpressed. Regardless of how much Sophie would whine, he'd have him out by Christmas, once the whole ridiculous charade he was embroiled in had blown over.

Dickie gave a parting nod to the dour-looking girl in desperate need of a smile and more make-up, she didn't nod back, the lack of manners was astounding. Then he made himself scarce, anxious to finally meet the clients on the ground floor. His little pioneers, ready and willing to launch his legacy. He skipped down the stairs, his stubby legs breaking into an excited hop as he neared the A-suite.

His joy was immediately doused by the vile language being screamed from the other side of the door. He burst in. Eleven foul-mouthed Subs were closing in on the lab monkey (Dickie had already forgotten his name), so he ordered him out of the room to bleat in the corridor before things got out of hand. The Subs were still blindly revolting when Dickie re-entered. He turned the touchwall off and their Halos cleared. They looked around, then fixed their stares on him.

"Calm down," Dickie insisted.

"He called us bastards!" said one.

A second voice came from the back of the room: "Said we were animals!"

"He's a *shit* teacher, a right prick!" called a third.

"Less of the curse words, my boy," Dickie said.

"I'm puttin' in a complaint, get the prick fired. Who'd I complain to?"

"Have you ever looked at that immaculate portrait of Dr.Vaneman, hanging in reception?"

"No. So what?"

"Don't... don't you know who I am?" Dickie asked.

They shrugged.

Dicke shook his head, "*Do you know who I am? I'm* Dr.Vaneman."

"So what?"

"Lord, give me strength. *I'm* Dr.Vaneman. *I'm* in charge. Complain to me, boy."

"Yeh, well, I'm complainin'. That prick said we were bas-tards. You gonna fire him?"

"If I must, of course. I'm in charge. I never shy away from difficult decisions. You have my word, I'll look into it, and at the minimum, he'll get a ruddy good telling off." A few of the sneers turned to smiles. Dickie warmed to their ripple of acceptance. "… Yes, there we go, I'm not afraid to fire him if I have to. No one insults my little Subs. The man's in trouble. Big trouble," more started nodding. Dickie had them. He loved owning his crowd. It was why, once he'd acclimatised to the smell, he could appreciate Subs – they were pleased by the cheapest promises. "… Rest assured, a slight on you, is a slight on the CEO of this very institution, Dr.Vaneman… me. You, little people, are the most impor-tant things on this site, after me. You're the glue. He'll not get away with it. Mark my words, I'll scold the man. If it were a boxing contest, they'd be stopping it in the first round. I'll see to it that he doesn't have a job by the day's end."

"… You do the lesson, Sir," one said. "You seem alright, miles better than that prick. Please, Sir, you do it."

The group voiced their agreement.

Dickie held his hands up, "Well, I can't criticise your taste. Settle down, settle down. Of course, I can teach you… your seats, please." He turned the touchwall back on, picked up the Block from the desk, and had a scan of the presentation instructions. "It looks like we're going to practise National values lessons. We'll have a few run-throughs and then do it all over again for the cameras this afternoon. Now, it's impor-tant we don't overdo it, we still want you to come across as natural. But what is vital is you show the difference between what you're normally like, when you're... you know... *Subs*, and how you change for the better with CTRL. So, we'll also let you experience its effects, to give you a chance to get used to it. Like I said, before CTRL, don't be afraid to be your normal, Sub, selves. OK?" some nodded. "Good." Dickie read from the touchwall as it scrolled, "Today you will learn to recite, write and *believe* in the four fundamental values. Who can tell me just one?" they shifted in their seats. "Come on. It's written in front of your faces, just read!" they remained silent. "The four values... right in front of you... any of you... just read one?" a Sub raised her hand, Dickie strolled over and slapped it down. "You're a Sub, remember? Not so keen," he whispered, before raising his voice again. "The four values, anyone?... Anyone?... no-one? Fine. What do you think I mean when I say fundamental values?" silence. "What do you think makes a valuable citizen?" no response. "What should a Nation demand from its citizens? ..."

Dickie smiled and turned off the touchwall. When their eyes reappeared, most of them were shut.

"Remarkable," Dickie said. "Just remarkable. If you can all start the lesson off exactly like that in front of the cameras, later on, that would be perfect. You might even want to throw in the occasional crude remark. Any task, no matter how simple, you Subs find a way of avoiding progress – that's exactly what I'm after. OK, I've been told this next bit is a little ... odd. Just relax."

Dickie pressed the CTRL app on the Block. The logo filled the screen and revealed a list of options. He pressed the button to initiate the active Halos. Normally not a details-man, Dickie was thrilled to know exactly what was going on inside the whirring head-sets. It was the only part of the CTRL document he had found interesting – PG11, Chapter 2, *The Application Procedure.* A chunk of text Dickie had found himself picturing when any of his recent carnal escapades were in need of a helpful thrust.

Inside every pair of goggles, a small needle appeared from the inner rim. A row of Halo-covered heads leaned back. The tips slowly lowered in line with their pupils. Once locked on, it remained in position millimetres from scratching the wet surface, making rapid micro-adjustments with every flicker.

Two wires flicked up with spring-loaded speed and began spinning as they closed in, sliding under the top and bottom eyelids. One of the Subs panicked. She stood up, shaking her head.

"No! No! Get this thing off my head," she shouted. "I've changed my mind. I don't want this."

"Hush up, girl. It will be fine," Dickie said.

The wires pressed deeper, the spinning motion making her eyelids fold in on themselves as it held them open.

She begged, "Get it off. Now. I've changed my mind. Please. I'm not who you think. I'm not a Sub. I don't want this. Please."

Dickie marched over as she tried to pull the Halo from her head. A single blob of thick jelly splodged out the tip of the needle and floated on her eye. The wires kept it open until the blob settled into a thick film. She scratched at the

Halo lens as the stinging became unbearable. Dickie grabbed her hands, concerned she may damage expensive equipment and was instantly astounded.

Her skin was baby tender. And the smell! He lifted her fingers closer to his nose. The smell was exquisite, sweet lemon and herbs, and God knows what else, wafting from her soft flesh. He wanted to fill his mouth with the scent.

"Please," she whispered. "Take this off me. I'm not supposed to be here."

"What's your name?"

"Sally," she said. "Sally Simon. Please. Take this off. I don't want this anymore. I shouldn't be here. I made a mistake."

"The worst is over, my girl," Dickie said, guiding her back into her seat. "I'm sorry I gave you a little fright, but it's all better now." He patted her thigh and stepped away.

The needle and wires instantly retracted, and the Subs took a collective breath before erupting with jovial disgust. They all tried to shake the Halos from their heads and they pawed at their goggles, desperate to rub the claggy strands from their eyes.

Dickie looked at the Block. Red silhouettes, with the clients' names below, appeared. He flicked his wrist towards the touchwall, projecting the image up onto the big screen and into their Halos. The Subs smiled as they realised they were the silhouettes. Casey Richardson lifted his arm. His on-screen counterpart copied. The rest of the clients all started contorting their limbs, flapping their hands, and laughing as they made their avatars dance.

"OK," Dickie said. "Let's start the lesson again, shall we? But this time, with a little help." He pressed the 'activate all' option and the figures turned green. "Please tell me our Nation's four fundamental values."

He selected a character. Casey suddenly sat rigid in his seat and grimaced as his muscles forced him upright, like the chair had rammed a pole up the length of his body.

"Give me the grace to trust the Nation's council," he said, squeezing the words out.

Dickie nodded then pressed a new Sub, who writhed with tension before reciting the second value, "Give me the grace to follow the Nation's laws."

The next Sub, "Give me the grace to accept the Nation's sovereignty."

The next, "Give me the grace to revere the Nation's faith."

"Wonderful, Subs... wonderful," Dickie said. The four speakers relaxed back into their seats, a flicker of fear and uncertainty twitching at their lips. "So, you can read the values. Now you must write them. Pens, please." Dickie pressed an option and the Subs all picked up a pen, their hands quivering with the awkward impulse felt by their muscles but not instructed by their thoughts. "Good. Write, Subs, write." They scraped their pens against paper, writing the four values over and over. "And recite," Dickie pressed again. They all spoke in droned chorus, repeating the four values. "Tremendous. If we continue making this much progress, you will all be able to repeat and write all these values from memory... we're learning so much," he said, clapping. "Now, the next step, do you *believe* in what you're saying? Faster, please, and with conviction." He pressed the screen again. The Subs strained like raw throats trying to swallow. And then they started writing again, but faster. "And recite!" Dickie shouted. "Like you mean it," he pressed again.

The Subs raised their chins in unison.

"GIVE ME THE GRACE TO FOLLOW THE NATION'S LAWS..."

Dickie gave a firm nod, silently conducting them with a wagging finger. He strolled between the desks as they chanted, their blind eyes held to the skies, their hands scrawling his bidding, their willing mouths reciting with a pride worthy of the words. Dickie felt a faint jolt of excitement as he stepped back in front of Sally Simons' desk. His thoughts lingered on her open lips, wondering if she'd taste as sweet as she smelled. He slipped his thumb on her tongue as she voiced the third value and held it to his nose for a sniff – briefly losing himself in the fantasy of unloading the most splendid eruption. He forgave himself for the lapse and pressed the Block again, to give them all one last boost, have them bellow the final value, maybe he'd make them stand. It would look wonderful on the Broadcast.

Ten Subs stood, "GIVE ME THE GRACE TO REVERE THE NATION'S FAITH!"

Dickie looked at the screen, one green silhouette was still sitting with the name Bradley Sherrington written below it in block capitals. Dickie stepped over to the brute, whose hands were clutching his desktop, his thumbs white with pressure. He leaned in to listen to what on earth the grimy specimen was muttering.

"I'm... ... not... yours," Brad said.

Dickie stepped away and pressed the Block again. Instantly, all the Subs slumped into their seats and their heads slammed onto their desks. Dickie shouted for the lab monkey to come and fix whatever was happening. No doubt that useless man had messed something up, he thought, wondering if he'd ever tire of rescuing other people from their incompetence, just pack it all in and watch the idiots try and cope without him.

Suddenly, the Subs went feral, chaos filled the room, and he watched as the one with the sweet mouth slashed at the lab monkey's tummy. Dickie did the only thing he could. He ran away.

13

"WE'RE FODDER"

Ren sprinted down to the first floor and straight to the upper entrance of the B-suite, the sound of the stampede close behind. She got there half a corridor length ahead of the charging Subs and was able to get into the room and shut the door. Then the familiar sight of furious, begging glares appeared behind the glass. She pulled the Block from her pocket and held it up to the window to keep their rage focused. They snarled and threw themselves into the door.

Ren looked around. The seats had been rolled in. She stood against the back wall on the balcony created by the foldaway tiers, before venturing to the edge. The small separation between the individual layers made for ladder rungs, so she climbed down to the floor and smacked her palm against the red button on the side of the wall.

There was a metallic clunk, and a deep hum rattled the room as the seating rolled out. After the first layer had fully extended, the second tier slowly followed, pushing the bottom towards the front of the hall. She kept glancing up to make sure the Subs were there. By the time all twelve layers of the auditorium had fully locked out, they were still bashing against the door. She was ready to finish everything when a voice made her spin.

"Hi, Ren," Casey croaked. He stepped his broken husk through the gap in the stage curtains surrounding the room. There was a belt digging into the flesh around his neck. He had a dusting of grime and glistening sweat, and blood browning on the tattered, saturated clothing clinging to him. His tired feet didn't lift from the ground as they slid him forward. "Pleashh, tell me if you know where the Block ish. I can't take anymore. I can't control it. I don't know what I'll do. Who hash the Block?" his tears cleared a path through the dirt on his cheeks. "Pleashh, Ren, I'm begging. I can't shtop it. It hursh sho much," he blubbed. "I jush need the Block. Where ish it? You know me, we're friendsh, aren't we?"

Ren thought about sliding the Block to him, seeing if that would bring an end to it all. But she *despised* Casey. No matter how battered he was, or desperate he seemed, she couldn't trust a word that creeped out his mouth. When the rumours had rippled about her and Mr. Brown, Casey would follow her everywhere. For weeks, she had walked between lessons to the backdrop of his hushed spite, describing in nauseating detail everything he'd imagined she'd done. He'd wound himself up one afternoon until his desperation gave him the courage to follow her into the PE cupboard. He'd squealed with glee when he shoved her against the rugby balls and bruised her breasts with his tiny pinches while he ground against her, smearing his fringe into her mouth, begging to know what she wanted. She pleaded for him to stop as he whispered through giggles 'I don't want to stop. I want to do this.' And for a few brief seconds, she froze as the sharp, fumbling of his roving fingers left a deep, scarring sensation. Dean had walked in just as she'd been dragged on to a crash mat, so Casey had pulled himself up and skipped away, telling everyone how filthy she'd been. And Dean had shut the door, leaving her in the dark with the smell of used pinnies and a mortified hatred for everything people said she'd caused.

Ren fiddled with the Block hiding up her sleeve and placed her arm behind her back.

"I don't know where it is," she muttered, taking a step back. "I think it's upstairs."

"Liar!" Casey screamed. "Shhlut. Tell me where, you filthy fucking shhlag," his tendon stretched skin pushed against the belt around his neck, his voice bristled. "Give me the Block, you dirty bitch. Whore! Cunt!"

Casey clawed his fingers and pounced. But before he could scoop his nails into her eyes, his head whipped backwards and he slammed into the floor. Dean was holding the end of his leash.

"The Block," Dean said. "Who's got it?" he stopped Casey from getting up with a swift kick to the top of his head.

Ren fumbled it out of her sleeve and pressed the CTRL logo. Casey screeched. He snatched the belt from Dean's hand and scurried across the floor towards Ren. Dean dived for his feet, pulling him flat and cracking his chin into the floor. A loose chunk of tongue fell out. Casey's little green figure went red the instant Ren jabbed the deactivate option. He lay still, his face pressed against the floor.

Dean stared at Ren. She nodded, so he carefully lifted his hands away from the Sub's feet.

"Have I done it?" Ren asked. "Is he off?"

"Casey?" Dean looked at the Block. "Are you OK?"

"… I hate you," Casey muttered.

"You need to turn him grey. Press it again," Dean said.

"What?" Ren said.

Dean pulled the Block from her grip and looked at the little, shuddering, red figure. He pressed the screen and it faded to grey. Casey went rigid, then loosened with a shiver, then wailed. A big, whooping, honking cry, like a seal being clubbed. He angled his head up to glare at Ren before picking up his bit of tongue, dragging himself over to the wall, and bunching into a tight cocoon to sob into his knees.

"Why did you come back?" Ren asked.

"I dunno… bored," Dean said.

"I've done it! We've done it! We just need to go and let the others in to turn them off, and we've done it."

"Where is everyone?"

"I didn't need them. I did it alone."

"That's stupid! What do you get out of this? It's their fucking job to sort this. Where's everyone else?"

"Upstairs. They're safe. *I* did it, Dean."

"I don't give a shit if they're safe. Why are you on your own? Where's my aunt? Where's Mr. Brown? Why did they leave you?"

"Mrs. Burns is looking after that man, she *had* to. And Mr. Brown didn't leave me, he *saved* me, so I saved him... ... because I love him."

"... Listen to yourself. It's not you. Fawning over that bastard has ruined you. It's made you fucking stupid," Dean sighed.

"*Stop calling me that.* I'm not," Ren snapped. "And he loves me!"

"He doesn't love you. He's using you. He's just a filthy old man."

"He isn't. We never had sex. I lied."

"I know you didn't. That doesn't matter, he still screwed you. He leched all over you," Dean said. Ren swallowed. "Fucking giggling and whispering to you, letting his fingers linger when he stroked by. I bet he's said all kinds of shit to you. I bet he's tried kissing you, hasn't he? Said how special you are? He's fucking grooming you! I even told my aunt I thought he was off, that you wouldn't just make something up. But she didn't want to hear it, probably would have made things too awkward. She said I was lying. It's easier to blame a slag."

"We... we never kissed," Ren said weakly.

"Don't defend him," Dean said. "He won't defend you. None of them will. Not when it matters."

"Not like you, you mean? We were friends until everyone hated me. Then even you, the big brave boy who doesn't give a shit. Even you started giving a shit, you couldn't be seen with me. You're the biggest hypocrite of them all."

"It's because you went mental! Fucking obsessing over that dirty man… I used to think about you all the time. I remember laughing with you because something was funny, not because I was being a prick. It's weird that you don't even realise you're missing stuff like that – but you came along and not everything was dulled anymore. But you fucking lost it, because of that pervert."

"Is that what it was, you were jealous? We're only allowed to spend time together if I'm thinking of you? Are you that tiny that I need to be looking at you all the time so you don't disappear? *You* stopped talking to me, or sitting next to me… when you saw what Casey was doing to me you left me in the dark so you could go and hit him."

"There was nothing else I could do. What did you want?"

"*Not to be alone*! I needed someone. Unfortunately, I got you. You're no different. You only help if nothing changes. You only try and fix things by breaking them. At least Mr. Brown makes me feel good."

"He makes *himself* feel good. He doesn't give a shit what you feel!"

"He loves me," Ren said with a fresh burst of defiance. "He said so."

"He's not here for you, Ren! No-one is! We're fodder, labelled and sorted. They don't want us to be anything, they already know what we are. We're all getting fucked, you worse than the rest. Shitty Shoes is a fucking creep with a soft smile and dirty fingers. He'll bleed you. Someone as good as you don't need others to feel right – you were better than anyone I knew! Then he came and ruined it. You don't owe him anything. You should use that Block to ring the Crusaders. Fuck them all."

"You're wrong," Ren said sadly, trying to ignore the doubt, pretending she was happy with how much she knew she'd changed since Mr. Brown had given her that first detention with a wink. "You'll see. He loves me."

"I don't blame him if he does," Dean said, softer now. "… But he's a fucking ghoul… you can't change the way you feel about something… maybe if I'd stuck around I could have helped you. I know you'd have done that for me… I wish I'd done that for you."

"It's too late," she said.

"… I know."

"… I wanted to be a lawyer once… maybe a doctor… someone making a difference. Everyone I hate keeps telling me I'm still a little girl, but they're wrong. I'm old enough to know… to know it never gets better. The only chance we have is to spend our time with people who matter. People you can rely on. You were… a disappointment."

*   *   *

Dean tried to say sorry but the word stuck in his mouth.

They shared a silence.

"I'll let them in," Ren said quietly as she walked up the centre aisle to the first-floor door. "You use the Block to switch them off when they come charging!"

A deep crack surrounded the door, but the Subs weren't staring through the narrow window anymore. She pressed her face against the glass. "They're not here!"

Dean checked the Block, "Something's happening," he said. "Quick, look."

They ran towards each other, meeting halfway down the aisle. The green silhouettes of the remaining Subs flickered on screen, the connection too poor for them to appear for more than a second. They were crawling.

"Where are they? What do we do?" Ren said.

Dean scrolled through the list of options, but whenever he thumbed a flickering figure, the screen responded with an error message. They stopped crawling. Like bears swatting salmon, they lifted their front paws and thumped down. Ren and Dean heard a soft thud and looked at each other. They lifted again, thumped down again, there was another muffled clump. They darted their eyes around the hall, waiting for them to burst in. Casey was still balled up against the wall.

"What do we do? *What do we do?*" Ren said.

"I don't fucking know!" Dean said.

The figures lifted once again, all slamming their hands down, creating another muted bang. Bradley's avatar rolled back from all fours onto its backside, dangling its feet, like he was sitting on a ledge. He lifted his right leg and kicked down. A polystyrene tile floated from above. Ren and Dean looked up.

"They're in the vents! They're in the ceiling. *They're crawling in the fucking ceiling.* What do I do?" Dean's finger shook as he hovered it over the list of options.

More polystyrene ceiling tiles popped loose and floated onto the steps. Thick silver chunks of insulation dropped around them.

"Just turn them all off!" Ren jabbed her hand into Dean's back frantically.

Dean mashed his palm into the Block and started punching the device as it filled with 'no connection' messages. Ren stumbled back as a wire grate clattered at their feet, the final, flimsy layer. Dean looked up into a black square hole in the ceiling to see the faint, dark outline of Brad's smiling face. Dean smiled back, unable to shake the impulse to always hide whatever he was feeling. Brad roared, then dived, dropping onto Dean. The Block bounced down the stairs and skidded across the hall floor up to the wall. The other Subs dropped from the ceiling, some clattering with a yelp as they plummeted a longer distance onto the lower tiers. Ren ran across the hall for the Block, but Brad vaulted down onto the stage area, grabbing her wrist. He squeezed the back of her neck and shoved her face-first into the touchwall, then he lowered his head and stalked forward. Ren shook the dizziness that had been bashed into her and snatched the Block up from the floor. The Subs charged, so she shut her eyes and threw it. Dean clambered over the folded chairs and dived up two layers, stretching out his hand as it spiralled through the air. It bounced on his fingers before slipping away, over the back of a seat and into the gap below. Dean stared at the criss-cross of metal pillars beneath the tiers, a soft green glow shone in the darkness.

"Pass it here," growled Brad. Dean glanced over his shoulder at the Subs, standing at varying distances, all eyes on him, all thinking he had it. They waited hesitantly, itching to strike. "Give it to me."

Dean slid his hand into his jacket and pulled out his Aunt's Block, keeping it tucked under his stomach.

He stood up and held it aloft, "You want this?"

Brad tensed, fighting the surge of desperation. The wild eyes of the remaining Subs looked to him for a sign to attack. "Just throw it here, we don't need anything else," he said.

Without warning, the hall speakers boomed with the orchestral score from The Woodland Parable. The huge touchwall filled with the frolicking creatures as they skipped into the distance, their wagging bushy tales exposing sphincter-free backsides. The Subs' Halos blacked as the image filled their sight. They roared as one. Dean glanced at Ren, whose hand was still pressed firmly against the touchwall button, and smiled. Then he held up his hand and wagged his finger furiously between pointing at his aunt's Block and beneath the seating. Ren's face scrunched with confusion. Dean spewed a tirade of 'fucks.' He had an odd flash of memory, it was Christmas again, his mum was alive, she was pretending to be happy, and the worst thing that could ever happen to him was being paired with his dopey nan for the game of charades. His eyes bulged as he pointed furiously, mouthing 'Block under there,' jumping on the spot, as if getting irate would help. Slowly, Ren lit up and she nodded her understanding enthusiastically.

Brad dropped onto all fours and fumbled for the edge of a chair frame, patting the steel until he found a corner, then he smashed his face into it. The clang echoed. Dean, frozen with shock, watched Brad hammer his Halo into the metal until there was a crack, and a smattering of glass and blood dropped onto the back of a folded chair. Brad angled his head up to look out the corner where his vision poked through. Blood rimmed the goggles, trailing down his cheeks like tears. The Sub scraped a hooked finger into the small crack and peeled the lens away, leaving just the empty Halo frame stuck to his face. He looked at Dean, then charged.

Dean sprinted to the edge of the seating and jumped towards the thin metal side railings that housed the audience. He planted his feet against the top of it and vaulted across the gap, clutching at the curtain, holding himself up, mid-air. He shoved the stolen Block between his teeth, and hauled himself higher, grasping thick handfuls of material as he scaled to the tracks bolted into the ceiling. He hoisted himself between the ceiling panels and the metal curtain pole and looked down. Brad stared back. He walked down the tiered seating onto the hall floor, shoving aside the blind Subs snarling at the cartoon creatures prancing in their heads. He walked around the side until he was standing directly below. Dean removed the screen from his mouth and balanced precariously, hugging the railing. Brad wrapped a loop of heavy curtains around his arm and pulled.

14

BRADLEY SHERRINGTON

Brad pressed his knuckles into his bedroom wall until they cracked. The pillow between his legs stopped his thighs from sticking together, but now his head was too low. It didn't matter how cold it was outside, in the Paradise Flats, the heat would rise with the sour shit stench. Anywhere above the 5th and the air was so thick it filled your mouth. It was the mirror cladding. Most Paradise Flats were converted office blocks. The reflective wrapping signalled the new purpose for these abandoned buildings – housing the worst. But, inside, little had changed. Drab, fluorescent-lit expanses were filled with stud walls to divide the grey space into tiny living quarters. The cladding made the towers gleam *proudly* for miles around, but it was like covering a drunk's outhouse in foil, festering the humidity until it seeped from the polystyrene ceiling tiles. The dripping from Brad's back left a sodden line down the centre of his sagged mattress. He knew there was no way he was getting back to sleep. As always, the apartment lights had turned on with the four AM announcement to make sure his mum couldn't be late. Brad had smashed his bedroom light as soon as they'd moved in, but the repeated message ordering her to get up still woke him most mornings. He thumped his wall and listened to the scattering rubble falling behind the blown render and wallpaper. By the time he'd given up on staying in bed, she'd already left for her shift. She hadn't collected the delivery, which meant she hadn't eaten. He knew she was doing it so he could have more, but an extra pouch was no good to him if she collapsed at work again. It was close to impossible to get fired from the Lines, but it could *always* be more miserable. Disciplinaries increased your quota. And with no time left to spare, already saving precious minutes foregoing the dignity of a toilet by filling an adult nappy, an increase in quota meant longer hours. She may as well end up sleeping on the factory floor. His mum was full of useless gestures – skipping meals for him, staying up into the early hours to clean their vile apartment, doing favours for men on the lower floors so she could buy extras – he hated it. He didn't want the food. The apartment could never be properly clean. And, every time she let someone new use her, she was only adding to the list Brad had to cripple. She wasn't bright enough to know she didn't help – it was her only way of trying to make up for being his mother.

Brad stepped out onto the balcony and looked down. In his paradise, behind the shine, the building was a towering, hollow, concrete cylinder – a prettied old bone stuck in the dirt – so he could see the bustle all the way down to the 1st. It was busy – it was always busy – but leaflet days were particularly so because of the roach report. Mother Gabrielle's Boys were out rounding up all the nonces and pouch thieves that had been named.

Brad lived with his mum on the 12th. Back in their old zone, he'd managed to work them down to the 3rd without much effort, just running with the right people, saying the right things, doing whatever he had to. But since getting them transferred for slapping the teacher, he'd had to start all over again, trying to impress the new ground boss. He'd not seen her. She didn't seem one for show, but she ran things tight.

Her Boys started hammering on the door two down from Brad, "Fucking open up, Poucher."

An audience gathered. Punishment for pouch thieves was usually worth watching. Some of the smaller kids were play fighting with excitement, taught young that it's right to celebrate it if it's deserved.

"Let me know when you need any help," Brad said, giving one of them a nod – respectful, but not crawling.

"Yeh, will do."

They were the ones that would get word back to Gabrielle. Piss them off and they'd move you above the 20th – the lifts didn't even go that high. If the scum living up there wanted to leave their flat, it was stairs all the way – and that's if nobody spotted the filthy cunts on their way down. As Brad stepped into the lift for the ground, he heard the poucher's door being kicked in and screams being cut short.

Brad knocked on Mother Gabrielle's door and one of her Boys answered. Wiry and mean, his face so skinny you could see the veins pushing the skin circling his eyes. He had her tattoo on his bottom lip, so he was one of her proper ones.

"I've come to collect for 12-19," Brad said.

He stared, but Brad didn't flinch. *No matter who it is, or what they say, don't flinch. Don't give them anything.*

"You're down four pouches," he said as he handed over a box. "Someone got to the delivery before it came to us."

"Fucking hell," Brad muttered.

He was quick, grabbing Brad with both hands, squeezing his eyes and cheeks into the centre of his face. He clamped his teeth on Brad's nose. Brad didn't move, foul breath blasting up his nostrils.

"You fucking complaining? You fucking disrespecting Mother?" he said through gritted teeth.

"… No," Brad said.

"You fucking disrespect Mother and I'll eat your fucking face. Understand?"

"… … Yes," Brad's voice trembled with a raging desire to reach up and snap the man's jaw off.

"Good. Say thank you."

"… Thank you."

He unstuck his teeth from the bridge of Brad's nose and stepped away.

"Now, fuck off."

Brad didn't want to follow the order at the first time of asking, so he stalled, "Tell Mother I've got a Block. She can have it if I can talk to her."

"Let me see it."

"I haven't got it yet," Brad said. He'd done this wrong. To promise something he didn't have made him look desperate, like a coward, like some attic roach begging not to have his stump teeth kicked in by offering a suck. He blushed, feeling the eyes of the waiting queue prickle the back of his head, figuring him for someone small, like everyone else.

"Well fucking talk to me when you *have* got it, Roach," he pushed his fingers into Brad's throat, shoving him away.

Brad put the box under his arm and walked away, pulling out a foil pouch and squeezing the sweet paste into his mouth. He tried staring everyone in the eye as he walked down the queue, begging one of them to give him an excuse to restore some pride. But they all wore their shame like hoods, none looked up. He needed to get that free Block so he could start working his way down the floors. Someday, Brad would own the ground, and when he did, Tattoo Lip would be the first. When what you're willing to do is your only currency, peeling and salting that fucker's legs would be as valuable as it would be satisfying.

Brad got on a Jane bus to go to site. He did most mornings. The Janes never stopped him. He walked into site with a gaggle of them as they shuffled through reception, out of sight, before reappearing with mop buckets and glazed expressions. He watched them glide their chemical scent around the empty building. One of them kept trying to catch his eye, an old lady, waving with the tips of her fingers and slanting her head to one side with a sympathetic smile. She stopped mopping and waddled over.

"You alright, duck? You look lonely," she said.

"Fuck off."

She tilted her head to the other side, still smiling, "That kind of morning, is it?"

"Seriously, fuck off back to mopping."

"Ooh, salty, aren't we? I'd not like to see you in a bad mood."

Brad turned away. She parked her backside on the chair next to his, a tired elbow nudging into his side.

"Fuck's sake!" he said, scraping his chair away a few inches.

"Sorry, duck," she chuckled. "Got to sit more than the others. The old legs don't do what they used to!"

She lifted her left foot in front of her and started drawing circles in the air with her toes. Brad tried to ignore it, but he could hear her breathing and the creaking of her knee as she jiggled her foot.

"What the fuck are you doing? You've got work to do. Fuck off. And stop doing that," he said, pointing at her leg.

"Can't stop, duck. Set off the alarm if I keep it still too long. They don't care what I'm doing, as long as I'm doing something." Brad closed his eyes and let his head drop over the back of his chair. "It's not too bad really, as far as jobs go. I've had worse. I don't mind all the cleaning, gives you thinking time. I love a good think." She went silent. Brad opened an eye to peek at her, to see if she'd finished. She hadn't. "Over sixty years since my first job. Don't know what I'd do without one, to be honest. I like to keep busy. Always have. It's not much different from how it used to be, you know.

Nothing's changed. You'd think things would've moved on. But here I am. I had a mop when I was a young lady. I've still got one, plus a bunch of memories. You'd think with all the memories flying about we might've changed. S'pose that's why so many people are sad nowadays. But not me. As long as I'm busy, I'm happy. That's what my memories have learned me."

Brad sat up, "If you don't shut up, I'm going to snap your fucking mop."

"Oh, I bet you would as well." She laughed. "My first husband had a temper like yours. Lovely man, died of a heart attack. Big strapping fella."

"… You're retarded."

"Not like my second. He was soft and gentle, wouldn't hurt a fly, never complained. By the time the cancer took him, he'd let it get so far along without saying a peep, he was lumpier than a bag of frozen peas." Brad shook his head, then spat a chunk of gob out with enough force that it flew across reception and slapped on her polished section of floor. "Cheeky beggar," she muttered, laughing. She stood up. "Anyway, back to it. It was lovely talking to you, young man."

She started to wander back to her mopping, humming an old tune.

"How can you be smiling? If I were you, I'd drown myself in my mop bucket," Brad said.

"You never know what's around the corner. You've got to make yourself smile, nothing else will."

"There's nothing around the corner. What are you? Eighty? Ninety? You look a hundred. You're gonna be fucking dead soon. All your time wasted waiting with a stupid grin. You're fucking pointless! Go on – stick your head in the bucket! No one gives a shit. No one'll remember."

She smiled again. Brad wanted to kick her bucket over but he couldn't be bothered to get up. Her ankle tag buzzed three times. All of the Janes stopped cleaning and walked their mops back to where they'd got them, then formed a sad line at the main entrance.

The old woman waved goodbye to Brad, "Thank you for the lovely start to the day, young man."

"What the fuck is wrong with you?" Brad said.

"Nothing, duck."

"Well stop fucking smiling then."

"Why?"

"There's nothing for you to be happy about."

"Oh, dear. After the years I've had, I've no choice but to be happy. There's only one person in charge of how I feel. I'm not going to let it be you, am I?"

And then the Janes drifted away, heads bowed, back onto their bus, shipped off to some other carcass in need of a dusting.

Brad was left sitting for an hour before the other Subs turned up. He had to make an example of one straight away, and another was stupid enough to have a go at eyeballing him (he wouldn't forget that). But they all seemed to have an idea of who he was. They'd probably seen him in the National section of the leaflet from a month ago. He'd kept the back page as a souvenir. Not because he was proud, but because it was a reminder – fuck them.

No one can tell him what to do, or write, or where to sit, or when to eat. And some fresh-faced beaming bitch won't whimper about him going to the toilet. As if anything they say means anything when he's got to catch his grey bus back to his steaming tower, teaming with maggots. Its mirror skin would crawl if it could. When you have to stand aside, first thing in the morning, for a screaming poucher trying to hold his eyeballs in their shattered sockets while he's carried up above the 20th, it deadens the volume of polite demands from pointless teachers.

Keeping the peace with weak people that don't matter is the kind of thing his mum does. Nodding along, hoping it gets easier, always grinding, but never making any ground. Letting yourself get fucked in the ass so you can buy your kid shoes. The greatest gift she'd ever given him was teaching him what *not* to be. Working the lines was a wretched crawl towards death, scouring miles of shelves to pick up things to pack in boxes. The first minute *identical* to the last, years later as you keel over on the dusty factory floor. But, since Rego had convinced Ministers to amend the Joe and Jane initiative, the delabelled had been forced to swell the Lines' workforce, inviting an extra layer of sadistic, little middle-managers. Now it was tortuous. His mum would start her day dragging her belly across the concrete during line-up because those with the lowest packing quota had to move like the worms they were, or whatever other humiliation had been dreamt up to motivate the uninspired. And she took it. She just took it! Brad would never be told what to do. Not by managers. Not by *fucking teachers*. He would never do what they wanted. He was not theirs.

15

"HIGH AND MIGHTY"

Sophie paced the Bridge. She'd put Zach's clammy head on the cushion when she couldn't stand it on her lap any longer. His chest lifted gently with each weak breath, and he kept slipping in and out of conversations.

"We need to go down," she said. "*We need to help*. Who knows what's going on?"

Dickie stopped picking his nails, "How dare you to presume to tell *me* what we need to do. A team has been sent. At this moment, the last thing we need is a senior member of staff, and the *CEO*, embroiled in this... nonsense. I'm sure Mr. Brown has this under control, and if he doesn't, our team will be here shortly. The Subs can't escape the building, and they have no interest in returning upstairs. The right thing to do is to stay up here and not involve ourselves."

"What has happened here? What's gone wrong?" she said.

"Someone has messed up. Thank God it's only Subs and not proper people. But someone has messed up... and that someone will be dealt with," Dickie glared at Zach. "Severely!"

Sophie continued pacing.

Zach began flapping his arms like a posh, park drunk angry at the sky. "I'm ruined!" "Years of research. I put everything into this, all of it *wasted*. My father would be ashamed. I've made such a fool of myself, of his name. I do *not* deserve this."

"I don't understand, Zach." Sophie steadied his flapping by cupping his hands together. "*What's happened?*"

"He's delirious," Dickie said. "He's not well. Zach, save your strength, shut up."

"I was trying to make things better. Subs are a disease. They need help. CTRL is the cure. It makes them make the choices that are good for us."

"How?"

Zach squeezed a finger and thumb together and pushed it against his eye. "They're tiny," he said. "Little living machines. Made for a single purpose. The first generation was made in a test-tube... *creation in vitro*... by me...now my days are spent cataloguing the variants as the continually replicate. I'm working on a strain that cures illness, one that removes fat, another that builds muscle. The possibilities are endless. An army coursing through your veins, making you a better person without the effort, or luck, or discipline required. The CTRL strain alters the messages your brain sends to your body – it only works on the young, those with ripe minds – once Subs get to a certain age there's no altering how wrong they are."

"That sounds awful… bloody awful. How is this even allowed?"

"Spare me the shrieking! It's not awful, it's electrical signals, nothing more. It alters actions regardless of thoughts. They get to keep those. You do it all the time. It is your job to try and force Subs to change. You're just not very good at it. Besides, thinking anybody has any control is a falsehood. We don't choose what we think." Zach made pinging noises. "Thoughts just happen. You didn't choose to think of… … an orange elephant… in a wig! But now I've said it, there it is. We are all at the mercy of our minds. And a Sub's mind is damaged. They can't be trusted with the thoughts that manifest into action. They need to be given the right actions to become what we want. That's CTRL."

"But what does it do? I don't understand."

"Of course you don't!" Zach laughed, a particularly snorty sound. "You're simple. Don't worry. Most people are. Sailing through their daily lives, ignorant of the toil and genius that means they're not chewing raw meat in a cave. Subs can't direct their journey, so CTRL takes the wheel. They're still aware of everything as it unfolds, still experiencing, still learning – but their brain is a passenger in their body. Thus, letting someone we trust sit in the driver's seat. Without the driver, without someone controlling the app, it does nothing."

"But it *is* doing something, isn't it?… How? How is this happening?"

"… *Felix qui potuit rerum cogn-*"

"Shut up, you pompous turd!" Sophie snapped. "Speaking like that isn't profound. It's dishonest. You're too cowardly to face a simple truth, so you garble memories from your Classics lessons. You've messed up. Haven't you? There's no hiding it… you're simple! Don't worry, most people are."

"No!… No, that's not it. I couldn't have known. I deserve the benefit of the doubt. Years of work. I don't deserve this. I don't deserve blame."

"What about tests? Or trials? Or something? Before you pumped your bloody experiment into children?"

"*The clinical trials were a success*! … … It's impossible to account for real-world discrepancies. I did all I could. I couldn't have possibly known. Without risks, there can be no progress. It takes people like *me* to brave choppy waters. Not that I expect sympathy from the likes of you. The ignorant won't understand what I do…"

"What *have* you done?" Sophie said, shaking her head.

"Abnormal response – not apparent until outside a controlled environment. That's what I'll be forced to write on the paperwork before they make me pack up my desk," he said, his face so weak Sophie couldn't tell whether he was smirking or crying. "But it isn't my fault. After all I have done, all the money my father's invested. I should be collecting awards. Instead… … instead, I'm bloody ruined."

"I think *your* brave risks are causing more problems for the Subs than you'll ever face."

"*I had no way of knowing*!" he said. "I've selected and refined all my machines until they respond exactly as they should. But CTRL… in the lab… I only ever had the illusion of control."

"But how could it know? How did it plan *this*?"

"It didn't! Good heavens, you're dense! It's not a plot. CTRL isn't hatching some cunning scheme. It just is. It is the same for everything. Without a picture book, I don't expect you to grasp the infinite complexities borne of the singular drive to reproduce. Doe-eyed cretins marvel at the miracle of a newborn knowing how to suckle, but the ground is filled with the malformed bones of prehistoric infants. *All* miracles of existence are merely fortunate inevitability atop a heap of dead failure. There's nothing prescient about life. CTRL is no different. Its path is blind to the future. What it is, *I* have allowed, and it will continue to be, for as long as it can. Which, given it's such a *bloody* catastrophe, will not be very long. All my work will be consigned to a scrapheap. The trait that exposed itself outside of my lab will be the cause of its extinction, and the death of my career… I'm ruined… I'm bloody ruined."

"Did you know it might do this?" Sophie said, turning to Dickie.

"Don't be preposterous. I'm far too high up to be taking any responsibility. Even now, I don't have a ruddy clue what he's talking about. It's not my job to know. It's my job to lead. There is no one above me, so *I'll* make sure the correct person is held to account. And, you heard Zach admit it, it was all *his* doing. We both witnessed that. This is not *our* responsibility. All I know is, this was supposed to calm them. That's *all* I wanted. The only thing I care about is the data, and a projected drop of ninety percent for client delabelling is ruddy, bloody good data if you ask me."

"Oh, *God*," Sophie gripped a chunk of her hair, her voice ragged. "It's *so* terminal. This mass worship of numbers. NOTHING IS BETTER! We just altered what we measure. Too much poverty? Who cares, we'll change what poor means." She cleared her throat to steady a surge of emotion, "An epidemic of suicide? So what, stop counting the dead. NOTHING WORKS! Vile incompetence became a leadership requirement, and now *nothing works.* Do y'know, most of the data I send in is made up. I pluck it out of the air because half the time the computers in this building keep breaking down. There is nothing I do that is genuinely for these kids! They are suffering more than ever while I fabricate success."

"Oh, hush up with your repentance. Don't try and get all high and mighty." Dickie rolled his eyes and let his mouth hang open as he swayed his head in one long, slow arc. "What did you think CTRL was?"

"I didn't think. You said 'be onboard or go elsewhere.' So, I jumped on. And there's no excuse. I should have asked more questions, but it's easier to pretend you're not a coward when you don't know."

"Exactly. And I didn't bloody well know. This isn't us. We're in the clear, and I'll see to it we get a ruddy good apology and an explanation. Don't worry. Your job is safe."

"… I'm pregnant," Sophie said.

Dickie's nostrils flared as he steadied his reaction, trying to stifle the disgust. It was such a relief for men like him that since the reforms, pregnancy was no longer a safe space for weak sows trying to stifle scrutiny. It meant he could run a business without suffering the indignant swelling of a broody mare. But, given the circumstances, Dickie remained calm with Sophie. "I see... well... that would explain your figure. I'm pleased you're now being honest... eventually..."

"It was an accident," she said. "I didn't say anything sooner because I wanted to keep working hard, make you consider not firing me... and now I've said that out loud, I've noticed how pathetic I am."

"I appointed you GM on the understanding you were serious about the position... not that you wanted to play Mummy."

"I'm so relieved to realise I no longer care what you think," she said, slipping off her expensive shoes.

"What on earth are you doing?"

"I'm going down to help."

"You most certainly are not! How bloody dare you, Missy! Make the correct decision. Look, your pregnancy is a hiccup. Hire a Janet to look after the thing and I promise I'll reconsider termination... of your contract I mean, of course. Don't go down! Do not involve yourself in this in a way that I cannot defend. If you won't think of the good of the company, think of yourself... I will end you."

"Your threat won't work."

"I will. I'll end you! If you make me. I promise."

"You don't have anything."

"*I will cast you out with the roaches!*" Dickie roared, flinging off his purple jacket, the flapping sag of skin hanging underneath his arm, shaking his thin, silk sleeve as he raised a wagging finger – preaching damnation to cling to his pulpit. "That thug boy of yours will be on the Lines by the week's end, and you'll soon be squeezing pouch paste into your little bastard's mouth, hoping he doesn't vomit up another batch because you can already see too much rib through his dirty, paper skin!"

Sophie knew suffering. Having been lucky enough to drag herself away from her upbringing, it was a distant memory, but she had the scar tissue. She knew she could endure.

"Careful, Dickie," she said. "Your face is showing."

"You have no idea what I'm capable of. Do as I say. Don't force me to do this to you. People like *you* don't ignore people like me."

"Well, I'm pleased you're now being honest… eventually. Bye, Dick."

"LISTEN TO ME! You will stay in this room. YOU WILL STAY!" Dickie was no longer bothering to try and stop the spit from blasting out his mouth. "I will finish you, no problem, and I'll enjoy it. Oh, the pain I will throw! This is Rego you're dealing with. Threaten us and the retribution will be biblical. Don't force me – you don't want that. I can say anything, and it will be the truth. I can do anything, and it will be accepted. Do you think you're the first uppity little cunt to try and stand tall? I will destroy you. You all end up on your hands and knees, and then you'll spend the rest of your miserable days in a Paradise Flat with the scum and the sluts and the filth. DON'T MAKE ME DO THIS! *STAY IN THIS ROOM!*"

Sophie wasn't sure whether he was about to swing for her. His fists shook, but she didn't brace herself. She didn't want to tighten up the smirk creeping across her face.

"Nah," she said, embracing her old twang. "I wanna be good enough to care less about *my* survival. I wanna be better. I wanna be right... ... ya fat, fucking prick!"

She walked out.

16

"IT'S TOO LATE"

"Stopstopstop!" Dean said as Brad yanked his fistful of curtain. "Don't pull! Look, you want the Block? Fine. Stop pulling."

"Drop it. It's all I need," Brad's lips hardly moving as he rasped.

"And then what?" Dean said. "What are you going to do? Do you know what they'll do with you? The Crusaders are coming."

"It wasn't me!" he frothed. "It was them. That stuff in our eyes."

"You think they'll believe that? You're a Sub. You're scum. The science guy's probably dead. They're going to lump all this on you. Fight it. Control yourself."

"I *am* fighting it. Have you seen the other Subs?" Brad said. Dean looked across the hall. They were circling tight spots, clawing at their heads, Halos filling their vision with a snarling, cartoon fox trying to devour an owl stuck in a warren. "They're tearing themselves apart! Look at me. Do I look like I'm out of control?" Brad yanked the curtain again. "Right now, I want that Block. I want to drag myself up there and crush your fucking skull to a pulp. But I won't. Yet." Dean tightened his grip on the railing, the slide of his sweaty hands on the brushed steel created an unbearable tingling in his fingers. "The urge hurts, it's hard to ignore, but I'm strong enough to reason with it. Whatever happens, I know I'm going to end up ripping that thing from your hands. I'd like to do that without breaking myself in the process. I know you're smart enough to listen. I know you'll do the right thing and throw it down. And that's why you're not already dead. Because I keep telling myself I know I'm going to get what I need," he paused, took a breath, and bit into his bottom lip until blood oozed down his chin. "*But if you keep fucking ignoring me, I'll beat you until your fucking face drips through my fingers.*"

Brad pulled. There was a twang of snapping cables, and bolts pinged free from the ceiling. The end of Dean's curtain rail wobbled violently then started to sag towards the floor. "Wait! *Wait!*" Dean begged. He held the Block out above Brad's head. "You want it? Here it is."

Dean tried to ignore Ren creeping in the corner of his vision, desperate to hold Brad's stare.

"Why do you want it? What will you do with it?"

"I'll smash it,"

*   *   *

Between Ren and the right-hand side of the tiered seating, Subs spun aimlessly, swiping at the air and scraping at their Halos. Roland had started singing 'I'm a rat, no wings or silly fanciful things, just a rat' – the hall speakers boomed with the clap happy number. Ren edged forward, her eyes fixed on Brad's back, her path always out of arms reach of any blind Subs.

"Please help," one whispered, standing in front of her. An induction year boy called Godders. She recognised him from the scars running down his forearms. He usually spent his days being chased around site by teachers or trying to impress the older kids by zig-zagging a pencil sharpener blade across his skin. "Please help me." Ren squinted to see if his Halo was off. "I'm sorry. I'm sorry. Oh, God. GodohGo-dohuh…" his pleading degenerated into gibberish. She held her breath and ducked her head away from his outstretched fingers as she walked on.

Ren stood beside the opening to the inner work-ings below the tiers. It was covered by a curtain, held in place by a long line of Velcro across the top. She pulled it from its fastening. Godders swivelled toward the crack-ling sound and charged. Ren dropped to the floor as he flapped and bumped like a moth at a window. He stopped squealing and shook his head from side to side, sticking an ear towards any noise. Ren cupped her mouth and crawled behind him. Godders sniffed and dropped on all fours, his backside sticking in Ren's face, the soiled stench so unbearable she had to turn away. He turned his head until the dark lens of his Halo pointed straight at her.

She could see the faint inverse of a dancing rodent, her hair wafting with each of his heavy breaths. He drooled a thin trail up her jumper as he closed in. Then crawled away, begging his body for respite. Ren climbed into the darkness.

She strained her eyes, peering over the mess of thick metal bars jutting out from all angles. The soft green glow was coming from the centre of the black cavern. She stooped down and climbed through.

*   *   *

Dean wiped a drop of sweat that had started to sting his eye. "Why do you want to smash it?"

"Because I have to." Brad was desperate to try and rub away the pounding in his head, but his hands wouldn't let go of the curtain. "Throw it down, now!"

Dean held the Block above Brad's head and watched him quiver with anticipation.

"Just drop it down," Brad snarled. He yanked again, a screw rattled loose and fell to the floor below. "I'm not gonna stop myself anymore," he leaned back, pulling his curtain-wrapped forearm into his chest. The railing creaked. There was a snap as another ceiling bolt popped free.

"OK... OK, OK!" Dean said, staring through the gaps of the seating, desperate to see Ren. "It's yours," he let it fall.

Brad pounced and held the prize up to his face. He folded it out to palm size and started to bite down on the glass. An oily rainbow spread under the casing where his teeth were starting to pierce, but before he could crack through, it rang.

He dropped it and hunched over on all fours, answering the call with an angry slap.

"That naughty little shit hasn't come home yet," said Dean's nan. "Is he still wagging it? Useless little bastard. That's it. I'm going to fuc-"

Brad snatched it up and bit down on the Block, clenching until it cracked, filling his mouth with hair-thin glass splinters and a viscous grey gel. He used his hands to finish what his teeth had started, breaking it in two, then raised his head and stared into Dean with a watery venom. Anything human had drained away.

"That was the wrong Block!" he said.

Brad launched himself at the curtain, hauling his weight up, screaming, and spitting, and shrieking. The railing swayed, having lost its mooring, it swung from side to side. The thick bolt behind Dean started to creak and shudder, pulling at the ceiling. Brad was halfway up the curtain.

"Ren, hurry!" Dean shouted. "Find the fucking Block, now."

"I'm trying!" Ren screamed. A clang, followed by a loud moan came from under the seating.

*   *   *

Brad stopped climbing. He looked down, then up, and back down again, before dropping to the floor. He ripped away the material wall covering the opposite side to where Ren had entered. Light flooded in. Ren was nursing her face where she'd knocked her cheek into a cold beam. The soft glow from the Block reflected against the polished wooden floor, out of her reach.

Brad's feet took a step into the maze of metal but he seemed to restrain himself from venturing further, battling against his hands as they tried to pull him forward, eventually relinquishing their grip. He backed away and brushed the stage curtain to one side to reveal the red button, and pushed it. There was a shuddering clank as the chairs rolled back into the wall. Ren screamed, her yell drowning out the final bars of the cartoon rat's crescendo. The Subs responded to her like wolves to a howl, lifting their chins to echo the despair.

The beams surrounding Ren folded inwards, everything around her moved, or collapsed, or lifted. She scurried backward, clambering over thick bars, towards the back of the hall where the layers hadn't started to pack away. As the tiers disappeared into themselves, bottom first, it exposed the hall floor. Beneath the seats, everything became tighter as Ren crawled through the closing space, fighting for the extra seconds a few more metres would gift her. She squirmed through the final set of beams and pushed up against the back wall, glancing at the narrowing sides, the gaps too small to squeeze through now. She wedged herself against the bricks as the final layer closed in, praying that the metal would stop short. Everything blurred into the periphery as a single head-height beam grew nearer. She tried to stunt its progress by pushing, but there was no stalling the slow crush. It touched the end of her nose, so she stood on tip-toes and lifted her chin to stop it crunching her face into the wall. Cold steel pressed against her throat, holding her screams. Her lips tingled and the sound disappeared. She closed her eyes and mourned the last months of her life spent as a faded copy, flashing desperate smiles at the secret gestures of a lonely, middle-aged man. She didn't give her final thought to him. Her last moments had gifted her the clarity to feel rage towards his dogged attention. She realised he didn't deserve any more thought. Instead, she imagined the sounds of her baby brother, the squeeze of his chubby little arms, and the smell of his hair as he buried himself in tight. She gave her thought to him – slipping into the comfort of a cuddled bedtime story where there was *always* time for one more page. She found herself in that.

17

SALLY SIMONS

The smell of melting wax filled Sally's senses like a warm hug. Sweet notes of lemon and honey followed, lifting her head from her pillow. Her mother, Coretta, was whipping up batches of nail polish. Their home was always fragranced with something she was making. The empty jars and vials narrowed every path through the house, waiting to be filled with whatever had been bubbling away through the night. In a previous life, Coretta had been a university professor. Post-Nation, with her particular brand of expertise, deemed irrelevant, she was swiftly ejected from a position considered remotely influential. Which was just as well, given her desire to burn the whole system to the ground.

Sally walked into her kitchen to see her father with his huge hands outstretched and each fingernail a different sparkling hue, having the final coat of Glitter Fudge applied to his thumb. He would make a point of leaving them like that for the rest of the day. Anti-nationalist sympathisers had to remain silent outside of closed doors – Sally's parents had lost all their vocal friends. So, her father dissented by causing great discomfort to the sensibilities of those most loyal to *their* Nation. A six-and-a-half-foot brute, severely scarred from a harrowing disagreement with a group of Crusaders, flaunting fabulous rainbow shimmer on the end of his paws, made the small-minded foam at the mouth.

"Sit," Coretta said.

Sally sat.

"Hands."

Sally put her arms out on the table. Her mother picked up her right hand and interlaced their fingers, then straightened out her daughter's hand by pulling hers free. She did this a few times until she was satisfied that Sally's hand was completely relaxed, then once more for good measure. 'If there is ever a day I forget to hold you,' she'd say, 'I'd worry you'd choke and die in your sleep.' Macabre enough to never be suffocating.

Coretta dabbed a soft cotton flannel into a saucer of vinegar and lemon and scrubbed Sally's nails. She used a dry corner of the flannel to buff each of them to a smooth shine, then started filing, squaring the tips neatly. Once she was satisfied the right hand was finished, having inspected it closely, she started the whole process again on the left.

"Have you made up your mind about whether you are going in?" Coretta asked, pausing to allow the question to bear its full weight.

"Yes. I've thought about it," Sally said. And she had, knowing not to make a decision her mother was interested in, lightly. "Seriously, it's no big deal. It will probably be some silly test. It's worth it to get a Block."

"Marv, tell Sally it *is* a big deal."

"Sally, it's a big deal," her dad said.

"Nothing *they* do is ever simple. A Block isn't that important," Coretta said.

She stroked Sally's forearm before carefully pushing each cuticle back with a small, pointed stick. Then drizzled a sugar, oil, lemon, and herb cocktail into her daughter's palm and started rubbing with the same gentle vigour she used to use when towelling her wet hair.

"Bowl," Coretta said.

Marv placed a bowl of warm water on the table between them and Coretta massaged away the perfumed oil and granules.

"Towel."

Marv picked up the bowl and laid out a small towel. Coretta folded it over Sally's hands and took the time to dab at every crack until her freshly smoothed skin was dry.

"The commune needs a Block," Sally said. "You said so yourself. If they run tests on one of those things, maybe that's the way they'll prove what they're up to."

"You're free to do what you want. You know I'd slip poison into your soup before that's no longer the case. But you can't trust them. *Ever.*"

"Mum, don't worry. I never get a second look. I'm a slag, remember."

"Ha!" she playfully flicked Sally's wrist. "That is one thing we can agree on... maybe that's why you want a Block... so you can send pictures of your bits and pieces to all your boyfriends."

"Or girlfriends," Marv added.

"Or girlfriends," Coretta repeated as she scooped up a thick mixture of oil, honey, and wax, and circled the balm into Sally's skin with her thumbs.

"You know," Sally said. "Most parents would take it more seriously if their kid got them relocated."

"The day we take anything they say seriously, my darling, we lose," Coretta lifted the back of Sally's hand to her nose, closing her eyes and inhaling. A slow smile lit her face. "Be afraid of them. Be angry at them. *Hate* them. But, always know, they are a joke."

"I know," Sally nodded. "I spend my days listening to them. It's soul-destroying."

Coretta dipped a small brush in a basecoat comprised almost entirely of corn starch and syrup. It made peeling off the topcoat easier. It was a recipe she was still trying to perfect, the finish wasn't clear enough. Every ingredient Coretta used shared one essential characteristic – it wasn't made or sold by Rego. She grew or picked a few things, but the majority were traded with the commune – a self-sufficient group quietly biding their time in an abandoned retail park they'd renovated. She could have ordered a chemical-laden basecoat for little more than the cost of a couple of food pouches direct from the Rego Lines. Life would be easier and few of her customers would mind. But the thought that Coretta would ever compromise was violently laughable.

She quickly coated Sally's nails with a surgical precision that bordered on artistic.

"You'll be out soon," Coretta said. "By going there. By going to *any* of their sites. You're doing something far braver than me or your father could ever do. I admire you *every* day. You know that, don't you? Not long to go. When you get out, you graduate and smile. Then we disappear off the grid before you have to work *one* single day as a Jane. You never listen to them ever again." Sally nodded. "But, do try to not get us relocated *again*, it complicates things."

"It wasn't my fault," Sally said. "The GM hated me since I walked in on him unbuttoning Mrs. Rustles' cardigan."

"And the 'kiddy fiddler' protest? We'd not been in 102 for more than a few weeks when you nearly got us moved again."

Sally held her mouth open, feigning shock. When she'd chased Mr. Brown out of his room, all those months ago, fellating her pencil while screeching insults, it had been entirely within the remit of the crass character she had adopted. But the unnecessary attention it created was dangerous. Going 'off the grid' wasn't particularly difficult. The more unpleasant Ministers were, the more incompetent they tended to be, and Occupation Ministers were utterly malicious. But making a *whole* family disappear, even for someone as resourceful as Coretta, is a real challenge if one of them has been delabelled. They joke about it now, but Sally had seen a hint of the fury her mother contained.

"It was Dad's idea," Sally said, pointing at him.

Coretta looked at Marv with a raised eyebrow. He smiled and shook his head.

"Besides," Sally said, "I walked in on him practically forcing himself on that poor girl. Nobody believed me, they binned my statement. I *had* to do something."

Her mother said nothing, her face stone still as she stared. She didn't need to say anything, Sally knew – they needed to achieve so much more than *something*. One lapse could have exposed them and ruined everything.

Coretta softened, "You have a real knack for walking in on people at the wrong time, don't you?"

"Your mother's only worried because of our bondage fetish," Marv said.

Sally laughed until her mum's pinch focused her attention on a small glass jar, Summer Blossom neatly written on the hand-illustrated label.

"Pink?" Sally frowned.

"It'll be lovely," Coretta said. "And I want to see what it looks like with the stars. Anyway, it'll suit you perfectly… harlot," she smiled.

"I swear, one day I'm going to crack and massacre everyone," Sally said.

"Even me?" Marv said, holding his sparkling nails against his chest.

"Of course not," Sally shook her head. "Just everyone on site… and then mum."

"Good," he replied.

Coretta applied two coats of Summer Blossom to Sally's nails with the same speedy precision as the basecoat, then carefully tweezed tiny crystal fragments from a metal tin and placed them meticulously. She held up Sally's hand and admired her work. The crystals and glitter flecked varnish twinkled under the kitchen lights.

"Thank you, guinea pig," she said, giving her daughter's knuckles a peck. "They'll all love this."

Coretta would now spend the day traipsing her salon around the hordes of people that had worked hard to earn her trust. Of all her attempted endeavours, it was a surprise that this had been the most successful. No matter how desperate things were, demand for nice nails remained. She accepted a variety of payments – everyone had *something* of value. Her most trusted customers settled up by fulfilling Coretta's quota of gigs. Enough for outside eyes to assume she was scraping her family by like everyone else, without her ever having done a single minute's work for the benefit of *them*.

Coretta cupped her daughter's hands before she could stand, "You don't need to go in today. The commune will find a Block some other way. We don't owe them any favours. I've guaranteed our place there. Don't go in."

Sally laughed, "I think I can put up with a few Woodland Parable repeats. I want to do my bit. What's the worst that could happen?"

"So strong," Coretta whispered. "So precious."

When Sally arrived on site she didn't have to wait long for Dean. Having developed in him a soft spot for her, he was a useful shield. She just had to humour his advances and display appropriate reverence for his temperament.

Dean joked about her scratching down his back, not as vulgar as usual but just as boring. She giggled. He placed her hand high up on his lap. She tried to relax it enough to appear pleased, before quickly putting it anywhere else. She giggled, again.

These were the compromises her mother never made. Sally couldn't wait to get away so she could be the same. Until then, she'd keep giggling.

By the time the Halo was strapped to her face, and the tip of the needle was dangling its thick mucus above the surface of her stretched-open eye, it was too late. She knew she'd be doing more than watching Woodland Parable repeats. Her stomach flipped with the fear of what was to come. The jelly settled under her eyelid and her body went rigid. Nothing moved as her mind commanded. Her arms picked themselves up whenever they pleased. Her legs stood her to attention despite her efforts to remain seated. Her senses retreated deep inside, the sights and sounds blurred and dulled. The sweet cake and rainy forest smell of her mothered hands slowly departed.

Her arm reached down and gripped a shard of glass so tightly that her flesh opened up around it.

She wished she'd listened to her mother. She wished she'd stayed at home. The thought of her story ending before anyone knew who she was. The idea that her greatness would fizzle away unnoticed. That would be the worst thing that could happen.

18

"NO USE COMPLAINING"

Sophie slammed the door shut on Dickie's ranting and walked to the central stairwell, listening for the steady thud in whichever corner of the building her helpless Subs were throwing themselves against. A soft mewling stopped her on the second floor, but the corridor was empty. She ventured down, following the whine until she was outside Tom's room, and opened the door.

Tom was tucked into a corner, an arc of overturned desks forming a wall. With his eyes shut and his lips gently murmuring, he looked peaceful. He had Sally's long ponytail in his hand, gripped tight, and pulled through a small gap between a desktop and the wall. Tom was lying on the desk's legs, holding it firmly in place, as Sally softly butted her face against the other side of the barrier. Her eyes were shut, except for the occasional fit of fluttering, as her forehead bounced with a steady rhythm, like a toppled toy with a dying battery.

"Tom!" Sophie said. "What's happening?"

He woke with a start, grimacing as the pain returned.

"Sophie, you need to help. This one," he said, pointing at Sally, "she got trapped in here. I had to fight to get her off. I hit her so hard, I don't know if she's OK. Oh, God, Sophie… I don't know about the others. I don't know what's happened."

"Where's Ren? Is she OK?"

"I don't know. She made a run for it. I managed to get her in here, safely. We might have been OK… I told her to lock herself in the cupboard, but she grabbed the Block and made a run for it. I can't move," he pointed at the wet lump jutting out the side of his leg. "It must be broken, I daren't look. But I don't care about that. I just want to know if Ren's safe. That poor, silly girl."

Under normal circumstances, the sight of Tom's leg alone would have been shocking enough to break Sophie's cold calm. But all her attention was focused on the Sub on the floor.

Sally was damaged beyond the point of mere panic. Her limp feet were pointing unnaturally. Her trousers were soiled, the dark patches spreading to her knees, the colour and stench, in some way, more upsetting than her misshapen legs. Her top was torn and bloody, and two fingers on one of her hands were missing, the tatty nubs of blackened-red flesh flecked with specks of white marbling, like cheap meat. Her lacerated hands were peppered with splinters and glass, and her bloated, bloodied, swollen face was unrecognisable, leaving a smudge of red on the desktop she was weakly butting.

There was a gouge, half-hidden in the roots of her hair on the back of her head, only visible because it was oozing white bubbles that separated from the foam to float on the blood seeping down her neck. Despair clenched the breath in Sophie's throat.

"Sally?" Sophie whispered.

The Sub scrabbled to face the sound, like a crab rearing to avoid capture. She pulled herself forwards, but so slowly Sophie only needed to step away to avoid her clawing.

"Tom, where did Ren go? Is she OK?"

"The ground floor, I think. I couldn't stop her, I tried. We were safe, but she let them in and ran. The door slammed before that one could get out. If she made it, she's downstairs with the Block. Maybe she made it. You need to find out if she's OK. I feel as though it's my fault. She's a silly girl, but maybe I was too hard on her. She doesn't deserve this. I hope she's OK."

Tom started weeping, but, unlike in the Bridge, this time Sophie didn't feel repulsed. She wasn't quite ready for admiration, but she could appreciate the emotion of someone she thought genuinely cared.

"You're a good man, Tom," she said. "One of the best. None of this is your fault. You're a *good* man. I'm taking Sally with me. Help should be here soon, just hold on. You'll be OK."

"It's been a rubbish first day back," Tom said, giving a smile so sincere that Sophie felt overwhelmed with guilt for ever doubting him. "Just make sure Ren is OK, please."

"I'm so sorry, Tom. For everything."

Sophie backed away out of the classroom with Sally in slow pursuit, leading her to the central stairwell. Sally's eyes were shut and her twisted limbs jerked forward, lunging unnaturally, like a half-crushed spider, broken but relentless.

"Careful," Sophie said instinctively as they approached the stairs, wincing every time the girl bounced her head against the concrete as she pulled herself down.

Sally's eyes blinked open as Sophie baited her through to the first-floor corridor, not wanting her to suffer another flight of stairs down to the ground.

"M... m... miss?" Sally said feebly, her eyes barely pushing open the swelling as she tried to wake from her nightmare. Her top teeth were covered in so much blood and gum that you couldn't see how many were missing. "What... am I... what am I doing? I can't take... anymore. My bones... are grating under my... under my skin. I'm not right. Everything hurts. I'm broken... will I always... be like this?"

"We're getting help. I promise. I'm so sorry, Sally. We're getting help."

"Am I... is this... punishment? My old GM said... when he transferred me... one day I'd suffer... ... and there'd be no use complaining because I'd deserve... everything... Is this it? Is this because of who I am? Who my parents are? Do you know about us?"

"This isn't you," Sophie said. "It's not your fault. You mustn't think that. It is *not* your fault. There is a great girl hiding in you somewhere, don't underestimate yourself. So what if you misbehaved. The ones who dish out all the blame are far worse than you. You'll spend your life being told what you deserve by those giving it to you. You'll heal from this. You'll get the best care. I'll make sure of it. And then you can start again. Be whoever you want to be, not who everyone thinks you are. We're going to fix you up. You're going to be fine. Better than fine. I promise. And then I'm through with smiling. Not while children like you end up like this. I'm through with pretending I'm weak. Too many have ended up victims to the flaccid, groping men I've convinced are the smartest fat white sacks alive."

"What am I gonna do?" Sally blubbed. "I'm a mess... my body's a mess... I won't be able to do anything... I... I might as well be dead."

"I'll fix this. I promise... do you hear that? *I promise I will fix you!*"

Sally's eyes rolled into her head as she fought the urge pulling her forward. She yelped, her spidery crawl halting as her head stuck against the floor.

"Ow! Miss! Help!" she begged.

"What's happened? What's going on?" Sophie took a careful step closer.

"My hair, it's stuck on something, a chunk of it. OW! NO! I'm going to rip it off. No, Miss, please!"

Sophie stepped closer still, standing over the misshapen child, her ankles within reach if the Sub wanted to grab.

"Sally, promise you won't do anything. I want to help. Promise me."

"I promise, Miss, I do. I can control it, I swear. Please help, my head's starting to pull away." The Sub went red as her face tensed. She grasped at a handful of her hair and tried to pull it from its roots. "*Please, no!*"

"Shhh, OK, OK," Sophie said. She dropped to her knees and slowly slid her arm across the floor, next to Sally's mouth, the fine hairs on her forearm brushing against the child's swollen cheek. Sally didn't move. Her eyes shut to contain whatever was trying to burst out. Sophie stroked the girl's tensed fist until it relaxed, releasing its grip, then Sophie carefully pulled the clumped strands. They lifted from the floor immediately. Sophie realised the Sub's hair was never stuck.

"Sorry," Sally whispered. Then she sunk her teeth into Sophie's arm.

19

"STILL RED"

The tiers continued to roll back in on themselves. The skirt covering the gap between the bottom tier and the floor lifted slightly as it draped over the Block, Brad released the red button to walk towards it.

Dean didn't consider the drop. He didn't contemplate the potential for injury or factor in the possibility of failure. If he'd had time to think, he would've kept his arms wrapped around the curtain rail. Any decision Dean was able to ponder was always spoilt by spite, but the good still escaped with the occasional impulse. He let go of the railing and plunged. His knees slammed into Brad's back and they collapsed in a heap. Brad wheezed, his ribcage having borne the brunt of the impact with a crunch, but his body picked him up and walked him towards the glowing Block in the middle of the hall.

Dean smashed his shoulder into Brad, sending him sprawling again, and kicked the Block back under the seating.

As Brad turned, Dean crumpled his nose with a right hook, like a hammer flattening wet steak. Brad's head flopped back, but his body stayed upright. The Sub ploughed forward, but much like when Dean sparred first-timers, the movement was telegraphed – ripe for punishment. He sidestepped the cumbersome dive and volleyed a passing knee. Brad fell, and Dean didn't pause for breath as he swung full kicks, his toes buckling with each sharp thud. He kicked the middle of Brad's back, hoping to feel it break. He kicked until the deep growing burn in his thigh loosened his leg to jelly. He stepped away and gulped with exhaustion. Without Brad's body taking charge, the pain would have kept the Sub floored, but anything can be endured when you have no say. Brad stood up.

Dean snapped a jab below his cheekbone, followed by a hook into his ribs, before dropping him with a sweeping kick. Brad stood up, again. Dean punched him so hard he felt a finger break, then stepped back and booted him in the groin. Brad yelled in agony and spewed down his front, splattering chunks over the floor. But he charged. Again.

Dean tried another hook to keep knocking sense out of the lumbering hulk. But he was sapped of anything solid at the end of his reach, his knuckles only grazing the Sub's chin, exposing his back. Brad wrapped him in a hug, squeezing Dean's right arm against his neck, a useless hand flapping up to the ceiling. Brad squeezed while Dean tried to elbow himself loose with his left.

"Stop hitting me," Brad whispered. Dean kept swinging, hoping one hard, jagged contact would free him, but it was pointless. "Stop it," he said again. Dean stopped. Brad pulled him to the floor, toppling him under his weight, and leaned in, warm blood dripped from his mangled face, spattering the back of Dean's head. "I *could* stop myself, but I won't. Remember smiling at me this morning? Do you remember? That fucking cocky grin, like *I'm* some kind of prick you can eyeball? I let a cunt like you do a thing like that, I've got nothing left."

A white-hot sear soared through Dean's body as Brad sank his teeth into the back of his neck. The Sub clenched his jaw, snorting breath through his broken nose as he tried to tear away a slab. Dean's ears filled with snarling as the tight stretching of the skin on his back snapped loose and the gaping wound filled with raw cold. Brad pulled his head away and let the flesh drop from his mouth. Before Dean could honour the oozing sinkhole with a cry, his face gurned rigid, and his body shuddered stiff. A cold wave surged from the bite hole, through his limbs, before crashing into the top of his skull and becoming a prickling heat, creeping from the neck down, paralysing every muscle.

Brad stood up and scanned the floor for the green glow, but the colours from the closing credits of The Woodland Parable bounced around the room. He shoved a blind Sub to one side and kicked the touchwall button. The hall fell silent and the Subs stopped swinging, their Halos clear again. Brad dropped to his hands and knees, and they all copied, swaying their heads in search.

"I kicked it under there," Dean croaked, overcome with sudden desperation to help them find the Block. He had no control of his arm as it shot out and pointed at the seats. "It's under there."

The Subs ran to the side of the tiers. The gap was too small for any of them to squeeze through. Ren's body hung limp against the beams, her arms pinned up, her chin resting on metal. The Subs scurried to the button on the wall, moving with purpose, but lacking thought, all of them slapping at it until Brad barged them aside and slammed it. The seats started to roll back out.

*   *   *

As soon as the Subs were back out of sight, Ren opened her eyes. No matter how hard she pulled, she couldn't free herself, and she could barely swallow, but the bar had stopped short of crushing her neck. She heard the clunk of turning cogs and waited to feel the first movement. The beams slowly unfolded, allowing Ren to take her first full breath since being pinned. She pulled her arms loose and climbed, traversing the hunks of steel as they pushed forwards. The Subs stuck their heads into the widening gap and screeched as they saw her clambering towards the green glow, flinging themselves into the darkness.

Arms shot towards her. Clanging metal reverberated as they crashed into the beams. Ren lurched forward and grasped the Block just as hands grabbed her ankles. They pulled her towards them. She mashed the Block with her palm and watched the swirling CTRL logo load. Brad kicked a space between the scrabbling frenzy and straddled her legs.

"Stop struggling," he said. "It will be quick. No point fighting. Let it happen," he pulled her calf up to his teeth. She kicked herself free and scrabbled backwards. "Lie still you fucking silly girl. Let me do this."

She froze, "… OK… OK… I'll be still. I will. I promise," she whimpered in her familiar broken tone. "Just, please, be quick… please." The corner of her eye fixed on the screen in her hand as it filled with the Subs' silhouettes.

Brad leaned forward, mouth open, pleased at not having to hold her steady – a lifetime of fighting for fear had taught him to enjoy the frightened. The Block's soft glow pulsed neon. Ren pulled her leg back and smashed a heel into his chin. A tooth dropped from his mouth and she jammed her thumb against the screen. Every Sub slumped to the floor as the figures turned red. Brad collapsed on top of her, his face next to hers, unable to turn his tormented gaze away.

She dragged herself from under the loathsome weight and climbed out from below the seating. The Subs twitched and writhed as they tried wrestling back control of their bodies. Having lost it for so long, the sensation was slow to return, like a tourniquet had been removed but their prickling, limp limbs were still lifeless. Ren attached the material wall back to its Velcro fastening, hiding them away, whimpering and foetal, like closing the lid on an abortion clinic bin.

Dean was sitting on the front row, gingerly peeling his shirt from the tacky hole on the back of his neck. She sat next to him. It took a few awkward seconds but eventually, he placed a hand on hers, not because he thought she needed comfort, but because *he* did.

"I lost it. When he bit me, I lost it. I knew what I was doing but I couldn't stop, like I was watching myself as I sent them all in after you… … sorry… I'm sorry about everything… sorry I didn't stay with you in the PE cupboard. I didn't know what to say. It was easier to hit someone."

"I didn't want you to say anything. I just didn't want to be alone."

"Yeh… I know… I didn't know how to be alone with you." His tone changed, a hint of anger, "It's just the way Browny changed you. I had to switch off."

"Because I wasn't what you wanted?" she snapped. "That's it? Forget about me if I'm no use? I'm sick of feeling like I'm only worth what some *boy* can take away. The same *boys* who squeal when they think they're being ignored, or throw a tantrum if they go unseen. The same *fucking boys* who pull hair and chuck chairs the moment they feel undervalued. I was strong once. Not nasty, but fierce when I needed to be. I know I was, and I loved it… I'll get it back. I don't care anymore that no one helped. I don't need help… but I know I *deserved* help."

"… I'm sorry… I'm ashamed at how much it has taken for me to admit how shit I've been to you," Dean said. "You're worth more than I've got. You are… you might not need anyone… but I do," he stared at her, hoping for a smile, but got nothing. Then he carried on, regardless of whether she'd reject him, "You want to be mates again? Please? I'm better with you around."

"I don't know… … you're a dick, even when we're mates." Ren smiled.

"Yeh," he said, before interrupting the warmth with a sudden thought. "You need to hit the button again. Turn them grey. They're still red. They can still be turned back on unless you make them grey."

Ren scrolled down the Block and stood up, letting Dean's hand flop.

"Where's Sally?" she said, alarmed. "Sally isn't off yet. She's still green. Where is she?"

There was a scream from the first-floor corridor. Ren and Dean dashed up the aisle and opened the door. Sophie was on the floor with Sally's teeth clamped on her calf. The Sub was trying to bite through a mouthful of muscle. Sophie had stuck both her hands in the girl's jaw to stop her from closing the bite. Thick lines of blood were streaming from a flap on Sophie's forearm, a dripping patterned sleeve down to her hand. The rolling struggle between them had streaked long red smears over the polished floor. Ren looked at Sally's green figure flashing on and off-screen.

"We need to drag her into the suite to turn her off. Get her!" Ren said, shoving Dean. She stepped back onto the top-tier balcony, Block ready.

Dean thrust his hands into Sally's mouth, "Sally, you've got to stop, please. Or I'm going to break it."

She tried screaming, the desperate noise barely escaping from the gaps not crammed with fingers and flesh.

"PLEASE! STOP!" Dean begged.

Sally's eyes darted up, a part of her Dean still recognised, begging him not to do it. But she dug her remaining pink nails into his wrist and her jaw clenched. He loosened his arms, then yanked down with a powerful jerk. The curve of her jawbone clunked to the side with a loud pop. Her mouth hung loose. Her eyes turned to white. Her flailing limbs scraped in the blood.

Dean pushed his head into Sally's back and wrapped his arms around her waist. He picked her up with ease and stepped into the suite, dropping her on the top tier, before going back out to the corridor to tend to his aunt. The mangled body pushed itself up and crawled towards Ren's loud taunts.

Sally's body pulled itself down the stairs with a bump, spitting at Ren as she backed away. Ren pressed the Block, turning her red. She pressed it again and put the Block in her pocket as the silhouettes faded to grey.

The room, finally free, echoed with screams. Children staring at their gaping wounds, too terrified to look at the parts that hurt the most, gripped by panting shock. Sally remained silent, her body draped down the stairs, tiny crystals shimmering on her fingertips. Brad quietly dragged himself out from under the seating and to the stage area, where he fell to the floor in front of the touchwall. He looked up at Ren, his face too battered to tell where it was broken. He stared. She didn't look away. She didn't flinch. When he was too tired to keep his head held up, he closed his eyes and gently dropped it against the floor. Ren calmed in the quiet, finding peace in a moment alone.

*   *   *

Dean helped his aunt to her feet.

"Dean!" She said. "You came back. Why?"

"I dunno," he pulled his hands away from Sophie's, who hadn't let him go since he helped her up.

"I'm so proud of you for coming back," she said. Dean shushed her, giving thought to opening his hand out so she could hold it again, but it remained a thought, his hand stuck stiff against his side. "Why *did* you come back?"

"I stole your Block," he said. "Nan kept ringing... she was doing my fucking head in."

She put her arm around him, pulling him in for a proper hug.

"I have something I need to sort here, something I have to collect before it's too late, but then it's all going to be different, I promise," she said. "I'd like to come and have tea with you and mum tonight. I'll bring fresh apples so she can make a tart. Sound good?"

"Yeh." Dean took a step back before he could relax under the hug. "... Whatever."

20

MR. DREXLER

Mr. Drexler sank into his chair – a rare, unseen departure from stiff discipline. Then he sat up straight to take Dickie's call. Listening to that bag of wind was a small price to pay for a chance to return to the leather and wood smell of his dark office, away from the stretched-smiled dignitaries being greased downstairs. The soirees were happening almost weekly now. The price to pay to become a minister – canapes, crude chatter, and an entourage of fresh-faced up-and-comers talking too quickly and sniffing back the bitter taste they'd snorted into the back of their throats. It was a game for them, all a joke, but their punchlines carried weight. None had any real principles beyond hooraying whoever provided the next jolly. Mr. Drexler knew this, he had their files, studied their activities, listened in on their lives. They were all chaff.

He pressed a button on his desk, "My Janet?"

"Yes, Sir," the speaker replied.

"I'm ready. Put Vaneman through. Monitor and minute."

"Yes, Sir."

The speaker crackled as it connected. Dickie was breathing heavily, waiting to vent.

"… … Mr. Drexler?… This is a real, ruddy panic over here. We are all over the chuffing place. We have a room full of bashed-up, bloody Subs; the only reason they aren't screaming the site down is because they're doped up to the eyeballs and locked in a room with The Woodland Parable. Some of them are in bad shape. We had no choice but to sneak three out of the fire exit, so, God forbid, if the worst happens, it isn't on company grounds. And the rest of the mangled little critters are hidden away until the broadcasters have cleared out…"

Dickie continued whinging. Mr. Drexler let his attention wander to his reflection in the mirror. He looked good. Clean shave and crisp white collar aside, he looked like he did when he was in his sixties – the age showing, but only in a way that added an air of experience. He should have been staring at the bagged eyes and flaking, liver-spotted scalp of a body close to collapse, shedding its final decay in the yellow fingernails and foetid breath. For so long he'd watched with dread, the small, sagging changes of creeping weakness, as a life shorn of vice still succumbed to age… and then along came Noblie-Goggins with his miracle dose. A fresh reflection would only hide the parts of Mr. Drexler that would continue to age, Zach had warned, but while he waited on Zach to solve *that* problem, he appreciated how good he looked.

His attention drifted back to Dickie's incessant whine, "... And *now* there are two members of staff waiting for instruction, a half-dead lab monkey, a group of broadcasters standing in reception, and *the* most obnoxious mongrel I have ever dealt with, threatening bloody murder. How on Earth am I supposed to handle this on my own? It's not professional. It's a bloody shambles is what it is. You know I'm not one to need help, but we're in this sodding mess together. So, step up. Mark my words, heads need to roll, starting with that useless Zachary character, he admitted fault. A ruddy, bloody shambles."

Mr. Drexler paused long enough to make sure Dickie had finished.

"It's under control," he said slowly. "The team's on-site, you're no longer responsible. Confidentiality will be cheap. Take me to the ones causing a problem."

"… Good… yes, good… thank you. As it should be," Dickie said. "Apologies for losing my temper. But you know I only accept the best… perfectionist… yes. Good! We make such a formidable team, you and I. Formidable. We are the glue tha-"

"Vaneman, be quiet. Take me to the ones causing the problem."

"Yes, of course."

He was pleased to hear Dickie calm. The bloated sycophant made him feel unwell at the best of times, but his panicked snorts were inducing genuine nausea.

There was the sound of a door opening, then shouting. "I'm sick of this shit, it's about time someone did the right thing!"

"I know, Tom, but let's stay calm."

Dickie coughed an interruption, "I'm sure you can hear," he said. "Things are getting out of hand. As ever, your clear thinking in-"

"Shush, Dickie," Mr. Drexler said.

"… Yes, of course," Dickie replied. "I'll put Mr. Brown on, a Mid Maths teacher, just returned from a prolonged absence. Then it will be Mrs. Burns, GM of site 102; she and I have had our differences today. She's been on the wrong end of a few of my notorious tongue lashings. She is a feisty little birdie, but brilliant. She's my rock, and she thinks very highly of me also… … they both know everything."

"Mr. Brown?" Mr. Drexler said.

"Yes."

Mr. Drexler unfolded his Block to monitor size and placed it on the stand on his desk. It was filled with Tom Brown's file. Tabs packed with details: finance, search history, locations, habits, routines, diet, messages, conversations, photos, videos, calendar… everything. Whatever could be stored, was. And, when distilled through an algorithm and presented as a list of succinct descriptors selected from a database, it told of everything he was, and anything he might become. Mr. Drexler huffed a tired sigh, a sheer lack of surprise at the teacher's secret predilections. A mere glimpse at the sullied entirety of this man and Mr. Drexler knew how little he needed to offer.

"As a Rego family member, you are obliged to act in our best interests," Mr. Drexler said. "We are keen to keep you in our family. Given your conduct today, I'm sure Dickie will make a position available on the top floor. Are you interested?"

He grew tired of the silence and was ready to threaten dismissal when Dickie spoke. "He's nodding! Mr. Brown is nodding... good decision... great decision! Thank you, Mr. Brown."

"Mrs. Burns?" Mr. Drexler said, accessing her file. She wouldn't be quite so easy, he thought.

"Yeh."

"As a Rego family member, you are ob-"

"Spare me," she interrupted. "This isn't the first time I've heard that."

"... Well? Do you wish to remain a member of this family?" Anticipating further silence, Mr. Drexler selected her vitals tab, a list of real-time details to give him the edge in any stand-off – heart rate, perspiration, posture, breathing. Instant analysis of what any deviation from the norm suggests. Sophie's readings were blank, given that she wasn't dead, it meant she wasn't carrying her Block. Mr. Drexler would've been frustrated were it not for a glaring piece of information on her personal tab.

"She's pregnant," Dickie interrupted triumphantly, as if he'd ever be capable of telling Mr. Drexler something he didn't already know.

An argument babbled through the speaker.

"Mrs. Burns," Mr. Drexler said. The argument continued. "MRS. BURNS!" the argument stopped. "Stay off for six months. Full pay. And a guaranteed return to post. I'm sure Vaneman will grant this offer. He'll keep your employment status unaltered, so you won't be classified as a Home Mother. Would you like that?"

"*What a fantastic offer!*" Dickie said. "That is truly unprecedented. You know what?... I'm going to allow it... I'm going to ruddy well allow it! Such generosity! What a fantastic offer!"

"… …"

Mr. Drexler granted her the brief pause, already knowing her answer. He'd met her once before and been impressed, and her file confirmed as much – there was no way a woman of such drive would choose to disappear into banal, maternal obscurity.

"… … Whatever," she said, finally.

Mr. Drexler was no stranger to the sultry defiance that preceded compliance. Satisfied, he told Dickie to take him to the 'obnoxious mongrel.'

"... And a management position," blurted a voice.

"That was Mr. Brown," Dickie said. "I believe he is negotiating."

"I want a top floor post *and* a management position. Something easy," Mr. Brown said. "And full pay when I'm off while my leg heals – it's a real mess you know. *And* reimbursement of lost pay since my suspension, as an apology. Oh… … and Lauren Tamar… she's a stu… she's a client. I want her gone. Transferred… she can't be trusted."

"Do you agree to these terms, Vaneman?" Mr. Drexler asked.

"Yes, of course," Dickie said.

Mr. Drexler listened to the shuffle of movement as Dickie walked to the next room. There was a sound of another door opening, then a voice, "Why the fuck should I talk to him?"

He looked at the grand clock at the far side of the room, the steady circling a persistent reminder of the consequence of suffering fools, "Dickie, I am ending this call in one minute."

"Yes, of course. I'm ready," Dickie said. "We now have Dean Sandler, A Sub. He's also Mrs. Burns' nephew. And, Mrs. Burns, again, she followed me through, she's insisting on being present during this conversation."

"I ain't saying shit," shouted a voice too close to the mouthpiece. Mr. Drexler closed his eyes at the onset of a dull headache.

"No discussion," Mr. Drexler said. He didn't access Dean's file. He didn't need to. He wasn't about to barter with a boy from the zones. "You have two choices. Remain our client or be delabelled. If you choose to stay, Vaneman needs assistance with this afternoon's broadcast. I understand the other Subs are unavailable."

"Mr. Drexler, *please*, he's just a child," Mrs. Burns said. "Without him, things would've been far worse today. We should be thanking him."

"I won't repeat myself," Mr. Drexler said, circling his temple with his thumbs. "That will be all."

"*No!*" Mrs. Burns said. "That won't be all! You're just a voice on the phone. How dare you ruin things you don't need to see!"

"Yeh, you fucking rat!" Dean said. Mr. Drexler tried to dampen the boy's yapping by placing his hand over the speaker. "Fuck you. You fucking bastard. I'm telling everybody every-fucking-thing, and then watch you fucking crumble. I might only be a Sub, but when I'm done fucking shouting, everyone will know you're a cunt."

"Crude and predictable. Profanity has no volume," Mr. Drexler said. "Dickie?" he coughed away a tickling irritation, furious that he was repeating himself, "I *said* that will be all."

"Sorry," Dickie said, walking away from the blazing background dissent. "Mr. Drexler, what if the boy doesn't agree to assist in the broadcast?"

"He will," Mr. Drexler said, bored with how trivial everything was.

"But if he doesn't? He said he wouldn't."

"They say that."

"But… I'll look foolish… sir"

"I can live with that."

"… … Yes. Of course. Thank you. You're my roc-." Mr. Drexler ended the call.

He relished the thought of no longer needing Dickie. He'd read and listened to all his secret scheming. He knew of all of Dickie's little plans to jostle his way to the top. Mr. Drexler would persevere with Dickie until the vapid cog was of no more use, then he'd take great pleasure in ruining a man so transient in his convictions.

"My Janet."

"Yes, Sir?" the speaker replied.

"No more calls from Dickie, today."

"Yes, Sir."

"Another thing."

"Yes, Sir?"

"Mr. Noblie-Goggins is prone to overreaction," he said. "Have the following dictated to him the moment he wakes to ensure he doesn't do anything rash... *Do not be concerned by your failure. Surprising as the results were, it merely alters the timeline. I'm pleased with you and need you to continue your work as soon as you are able. You remain important to me...* Janet?"

"Yes, Sir?"

"Stop listening now."

"Yes, Sir."

He allowed himself another slump in his chair, the dignitaries would have to wait before he returned to honouring them with his fake smiles and dishonest platitudes – a departure away from his usual unfaltering probity. Something he would never allow himself to forget. A life of rectitude should have earned him instant ministerial approval – yet here he was, simpering like a quisling to leap their final hurdle. He knew the intricate details and appetites of every minister that needed to agree to his progression. They were all sordid liars, lacking the strength or vision to do what was necessary.

The zonespeople outnumbered the rest of the Nation more than ten to one. But they *had* nothing, they *gave* nothing – living on handouts and humoured with the fake purpose of unnecessary occupations. Rego had warehouses filled with machines, gathering dust, that could do any of the mindless tasks the Joes and Janes fumbled with. The sheer waste of ingenuity, the denial of progress, the maddening rejection of advance, all for the protection of something that deserved death. Mercy had allowed rot to spread roots, but the only people ever saved by mercy are too weak to deserve it. Mr. Drexler had no sympathy for the botched. And he knew, despite the Nation's steady embrace of the virtues of might, what *needed* to be done was still morally unfashionable. It needed *his* strength. Anything, given time, could be accepted as necessary – all cries die to grumbles, all doubts silenced by success. The Nation needed unwavering focus.

His Janet slid the printed minutes under the door. He found it comforting to have his cause committed to something physical to file away. It's the way he had worked for over seventy years. And one day, when the Nation was ready to learn of its saviour, he would be able to point to the precise moment he provided the solution.

21

DEAN SANDLER

Dickie was sitting on stage in the C-suite. The broadcast room of choice had been altered at the last minute for 'renovations' (a team of Janes had been bussed in to soak up the piss puddles and pools of blood in B-suite.) The camera crew was lugging around their equipment and picking at the trays of artisanal sandwiches and miniature cakes. With the chemical scent and piano plinks back in the air, the veneer had returned, completely untarnished. Dickie was alone on stage, next to an empty chair. 'I'll leave it empty,' he'd said, 'for when you change your mind and do the right thing.' The chair was going to remain empty; they had nothing to offer Dean. He was standing at the back of the hall, waiting for his aunt who'd been adamant that they couldn't leave until she'd collected a recording from the Bridge. He stuck up his middle finger at the seething CEO every time they locked eyes. The broadcast presenter, a swaggering mask of make-up and stiff hair, pulled himself up onto the stage. He gripped Dickie's hand firmly. Dean watched as the two men tugged and squeezed each other, their fingers turning white for the sake of hoping to convey formidable character.

"I'll do my intro," the presenter said with a wink, his hands changing position with every word, "then we cut to you. Make sure to pause as often as possible so, later on, we can cut in a flash-ad every twenty seconds or so. Don't worry if you make a mistake, keep talking and we'll clean it up later."

"Make a mistake!" Dickie pinched the bridge of his nose and grimaced, clearly horrified at the insinuation. "I think you'll find I'm rather good at this. Don't you worry about me. Concentrate and you might even learn a thing or two."

"Great. OK, where are the Subs? We need to mic them up."

"Ah... yes... about that... change of plan. I thought it better to turn this into a presentation instead of a demonstration. Less showy, more helloey... you know? Me talking to the people, clean, giving them what they want. Much better," Dickie kept nodding until the presenter relented.

"... Fine," he said, before hopping off stage for a final powder dusting.

Dean tried to ignore the tinge of guilt he felt for his nan. He could picture her, sitting with the bingo ladies, screaming and cackling at the TV, telling everyone how bloody gorgeous he was – she'd be heartbroken that he wasn't on. The house lights dimmed and all went still when a skinny man with red glasses and a cardigan with a picture of a dog's head, counted down on his fingers.

"Well, good day and welcome to our early evening broadcast," the presenter said, reading from a folded-out Block being used as a teleprompter. Dotted throughout his script in block capitals were instructions for every single movement and gesture. Without his prompt, he didn't so much as twitch his wax-plastered rictus. "I'm Judd Woodward. Today, I will be reporting direct from Ed Site 102." STIFF SMILE. TURN TO CAMERA 2. "Before that, here are your Nation's Hot Topics:

"Horror, as the zoned accommodation crisis worsens. Housing Ministers warn of the need to relocate citizens into the villages if their uncontrolled breeding continues," SHAKE HEAD. SERIOUS FACE. "*What. Would. Judd. Do?*" PUMP UP OPEN PALMS. "*Judd. Would...* neuter the worst offenders!" SHRUG. SMILE. BACK TO NEUTRAL. "Disgust, as an Anti-Nationalist plot to attack a maternity ward is foiled. Security Ministers ask, how long can we ignore their bloody ideology?" RAISE ONE EYEBROW. LEAN FORWARD. "*What. Would. Judd. Do? Judd. Would...* hang the lot – no need for a trial!" SHRUG. SMILE. BACK TO NEUTRAL. "Fear, as the crop crisis continues and pouch demand soars. Health Ministers warn of rising costs for fresh produce. *What. Would. Judd. Do? Judd. Would...* stop subsidising the work-shy!" SHRUG. SMILE. BACK TO NEUTRAL. "And finally," SLOW NOD. "joy, as the Perry, Perks & Drexler foundation promises to double its contribution to the Village Victims Relief Fund.

"I'm Judd Woodward, and they were your Nation's Hot Topics… A united Nation, is a great Nation," BOTH THUMBS UP. TURN TO CAMERA 1. "Today I'm with the CEO of Rego Education, Dr.Richard Vaneman, direct from Ed Site 102, to talk to you about an exciting new initiative called C-T-R-L. That will bring a little R-E-S-P-E-C-T to U and M-E," SMILE WITH TEETH. SHORT LAUGH.

"Thanks," Dickie said. "And you're right… I'm going to show you how we bring a little F-U-N to our lessons on FUN-damental values!" he laughed for longer than anyone behind the camera was prepared to sustain. His chortle died with a sigh and he stuck his thumbs into his trousers and pulled them up over his midriff. "Right. Start again. That wasn't my proper stuff. Don't use that. Are we ready to go? Let's go again." Dean caught his eye with a subtle wave, then let loose with a vigorous wanking gesture. "… OK," Dickie said, trying to ignore it. "Rolling, let's go again. Come on! Am I the only professional here? Rolling!"

"You… you don't need to say rolling… don't say rolling… just carry on," the dog cardigan man said, shaking his head. Dean finished his fake climax and moaned loud enough for some of the broadcast team to turn their heads.

"OK… got it… let's go again… rolling," Dickie said. "Years ago, our great Nation made the brave decision to be better. Things were terrible – we all know it was terrible. But, no more. Things are so good now, terrific, and nowhere has benefitted more from the change than in education. Believe me, I've been here, sorting this mess since the beginning – and things were a *mess*.

"We had children who couldn't even spell their names, trying to learn fifteen, *twenty* different subjects. It was madness. So Rego stepped in. We stripped it back – English, Maths, Fundamental Values, Occupational Preparation. The result? Things got better for us!

"We had clients, finishing their classification year with no direction or idea what to do with the rest of their lives. It was pointless. So, we created the Joe and Jane programme. We gave them purpose, we occupied them. The result? Things got better for us!

"We had *Subs*, ruining lesson after lesson because their lack of restraint is so ingrained. They are disgusting. So, we provided Halos to give them the focus their upbringing didn't provide. The result? Things got better for us!

"Things have got a *lot* better, citizens. But Rego needs to continue its approach to redefining education. Do you know why?" Dickie paused, pointing at the camera with a pinched thumb and finger. His eyes narrowed to convey the sincerity of a car salesman telling you something his boss *really* doesn't want you to hear. "We still have problems… there… I've said it… yes, we do. I'm being honest with you. Big problems! Let me introduce you to one of our Subs. You've read about them in the leaflets, heard about them in the broadcasts, but we deal with them *every single day*. I make no apologies for the footage you're about to see. Women and children may be tempted to turn away, but I urge you to force them to watch. Problems aren't solved by ignoring them."

Dean stood to attention as his profile appeared on the touchwall, his name and details scrolling across the screen.

Dickie glanced over and winked. Dean's stomach churned with anxiety, his legs tensing every time he nearly pulled himself forward to rush onstage and drop kick the fat bastard's head. He *had* to stay still, he couldn't give in.

The footage showed Casey Richardson tittering as he ran down the corridor from the PE hall. The video paused when Dean's furious face burst into frame. The slow soft whine of a violin started humming its melancholy through the speakers, a fitting soundtrack to the tragedy the audience was about to witness.

Dean knew what followed. After Casey had been released from the hospital, they'd been forced to watch it together in the Bridge – a way of exposing the foundations to rebuild their relationship. His aunt had demoted him to Sub when he responded with laughter. Not that he found it funny. He hated it, like listening to your own voice and hoping it wasn't you. He'd laughed because he wanted to piss off that filthy, smirking liar. And it had worked, because the following day, Casey brought a bread knife the size of his arm on site and tried to stick it in Dean's chest.

The clip showed Dean running down the hallway. The camera switched to a fixed view of Casey as he joined a riotous circle of friends and thrust his fingers under their noses – all of them whooping and humping the air. The violin held a haunting note as Dean sprinted into the shot, barging Casey to the floor, and stomping. He stamped over and over until the crowd backed away, the spectacle too grim even for their appetites. The music faded as Casey's hands flopped to the side and, in the silence, Dean crunched one heavy, unprotected stamp. He sensed the gasps of a watching nation. He imagined the outrage of the comfortably decent. He heard the embarrassed excuses his nan would've been shouting at her friends.

Dickie slowly shook his head. "Ladies and Gentlemen," he raised his chin to make sure the camera would see that he'd managed to make his eyes water. "... *that* was a Sub. Despite everything we do. All our work. We still have *that*. We can narrow our expectations, guarantee them a future, sharpen their focus – but no matter how much we lower the bar, too many still crawl under it. Until now. Until CTRL.

"An app created by our very own Rego geniuses, used to control miraculous little machines inside the Subs' bodies. When the Subs are angry, or tired, or rude, or aggressive, or just not working hard enough, our app makes them better. All those awful impulses they can't control, all the horrible choices they make, CTRL makes it better.

"Now, I'm not going to bore you with the science, but it's clever stuff, really clever stuff. Even I struggled to understand it, and I'm a smart guy, one of the smartest. But I will show you how great this app looks," Dickie flicked his wrist towards the touchwall to project his screen and scrolled through a procession of grey silhouettes as he bored the audience with an anecdote about his days laying brick. When he started talking about correct sand and cement ratios for mortar stability, and how ingredients are key in all walks of life, Dean noticed a solitary figure onscreen with a faint red outline and his name written below it. "... Anyway," Dickie carried on, "to show you how good this app is, let me click through to the screen with the fun stuff," he pressed to activate all clients, taking him through to the list of options.

Dean's body stiffened as the cold wave returned. His head slumped and the wave became a prickling tingle, crawling under his flesh like ants. He wanted to tear off his skin, to bite off his fingers and squeeze out the surging needles. His toes bunched in his shoes and his thighs cramped. Dean realised, during the moment Ren had turned the rest of the Subs grey, he had stepped out onto the first-floor corridor to be with his aunt. Resigned to what was to come, he chuckled… *serves you right, you soft prick.* Then he was paralysed. Only his eyes would move. They glimpsed at the outside world beyond the wall of windows running the length of the suite.

Ren was being dragged away by her father, pleading with him as she kicked the window and thumped his heavy back, begging him to believe her. She turned to face into the suite, beating her fists against the glass, the soft thuds getting the room's attention. Then she spat, a thick white foam, and punched, splattering it. She carried on punching, and a scream burst from her throat so loud that Dickie flinched. Her face shook and strained as she refused to let the scream die, her knees collapsing in the dirt. She started slapping herself, sobbing as her cheek reddened. Then her dad picked her up and carried her away so quickly that his Mickey Mouse tie flapped over his shoulder. Dickie remained silent as her scream turned to a wail. It was such a sad wail, like her breath was being stolen, the final cry before the seawater floods into an open mouth. A wail that, one day, when her father understands how wrong he was, would forever echo in his mind.

Dickie belted out a burst of laughter. "Sorry about *that!*" he said. "Some clients are beyond redemption, even CTRL couldn't fix what's wrong with that silly little thing." He laughed again, and the broadcast team joined in.

Dean sucked in a long, furious breath through his nose, and let it all go. The struggle seeped from his taut muscles. He stared at the Block in Dickie's hand and the thoughts in his head cascaded until a single impulse bustled all else away – *smash the Block*. The impulse stood him to attention and walked him across the hall – enough time to calmly reason with himself about the best way of doing what he had to do. He jumped up on stage. Dickie didn't notice until he was standing by him, facing the cameras.

"Dean!" he shouted with excitement. "So good to have you on stage." He pulled the boy into the nook of his steaming armpit and whispered, "you've done the right thing getting up here. All is forgiven. Right, I'm going to ask you some questions, you just give nice positive answers and smile. There's a good boy." He spoke up again, readdressing the camera, "This is Dean Sandler, the young Sub you just witnessed in that short clip. Not a good guy..." and he continued. But Dean wasn't listening – he was witnessing what his body was about to do, a passenger to its movement, unsure he would stop it even if he could.

The Sub reached over into Dickie's suit pocket and pulled out a silver fountain pen. He flicked the lid off with his thumb, and rammed the nib into the fat man's neck, plunging until his fist thumped into a flopping wattle. Dickie dropped the Block to the floor. Dean grabbed a nearby chair and rammed its metal foot into the screen until it spilled its liquid innards and the glow died. Then he shrugged and sat down at the edge of the stage.

Dickie grabbed the end of the pen sticking out from his throat, already slick with blood. He mouthed red, bubbling pleas that popped and splattered around his lips. Then he clenched the pen tight and pulled hard, and instantly regretted it. He dropped it and clutched at the inky, gushing hole. Dean poked at the broken Block, legs calmly dangling above the floor, as the CEO writhed behind him, squeezing his hands into his throat to try and stem the warm geyser. Mrs. Burns pierced the stunned silence with a shriek as she ran on stage. She ignored her begging, bleeding boss and cradled her nephew's head.

"It got you too, didn't it?" she wept. "Oh, Dean. Please tell me that wasn't you. Please, tell me this isn't your fault. It isn't. I'm so sorry. Listen to me. This isn't your fault, tell me it wasn't your fault. I'll tell them. I'll tell everyone. They won't get away with this. It's going to be alright. I promise. I love you. Everything is going to be alright." Sophie ignored the frenzied cameras swooping in for their extreme close-ups. She shoved away the caked face of the presenter who'd braved getting within arm's reach of a feral Sub to ask the burning questions. She just squeezed her boy as tightly as she could. "Everything will be alright," she repeated, rocking the child in her arms. "I won't give up on you. I swear. I won't give up."

Dean ignored a fresh impulse – the strange rush that lightens your feet at a cliff's edge, daring you to jump regardless of where you'd end – he wanted to bite her! He wanted to nip away a big enough piece of his tongue that his mouth would fill with blood, and then he wanted to bite her. He lapsed into a dark indifference, imagining her plea for humanity as he tore away a chunk and dribbled into the wound. But the impulse listened to reason and disappeared, knowing it would be welcomed back at a better time, like a nightmare forgotten moments after waking, ready to return with the dark. Dean relaxed into his aunt's embrace.

"Don't worry about it," he said.

"No, Dean. Listen. Hear this. I'm *never* giving up on you."

Dean thought about his mum. If only she'd left a note for him.

"It's too late," he said.

22

EDMUND STANLEY

Edmund screeched into his space. He'd already missed his morning briefing, a part of the day he relished, rousing his troops before retiring to his office. But some bloody mutt had ruined his schedule by jumping under his car. Edmund had watched the stray pant its last mucky breath. Without a collar there was no way of berating the negligent owner, so he had no choice but to shove the thing into a bush and get back into his car. This day was too important to be jeopardised by a clumsy mongrel.

The 'Savage Stabbing Sub at Site 102' story was still the first Hot Topic on the morning's broadcast. Edmund wasn't surprised. It was an entertaining piece, quite graphic, and a wonderful illustration to the Nation how deep the termites had burrowed.

He'd lost count of the number of times he'd warned Dickie about putting a woman in charge of 102; the site was too big. 'She'll be a pain in the neck,' he'd said (not a turn of phrase he'd repeat if he gets to give Dickie his 'I told you so' speech). Edmund had been the GM for site 97 for almost twelve months, after 23 successful years in the carpet business. Dickie had personally recruited him after being impressed when he'd given a generous quote, and the rapid progress he'd overseen in 97 proved what a good decision it had been. (Although it wasn't difficult to improve upon the shit that had preceded him.)

The broadcast had confirmed that, although Dr.Vaneman's condition was extremely precarious, a combination of his resolute faith and the Nation's best medical care, were contributing greatly to his chance of survival. The sheer girth of his neck, Edmund thought, must also have been a factor. Edmund wanted to arrange a meeting as soon as possible, he didn't become 'Carpet King' by being a wallflower. Now was the time to strike. Site 102 was rudderless, and Edmund knew he was man enough to manage two sites. After overseeing the introduction of the new CTRL initiative, he'd make a call to try and get a message to Dickie. Some positive news might help get the old boy's dick hard, he thought. Then he berated himself – Edmund was a Stanley. Stanleys don't celebrate sloppy seconds. Stanleys get their cake *and* the cream. With any luck Dickie *will* die. And when the sharks start circling, he'd show them all how big his teeth were. He quite fancied 'CEO' being added to his parking plaque.

He walked through the reception doors and was greeted by his Janet. She reeled off his morning reminders and finished by telling him that the site's email system was still down.

"My Janet, Sweetheart," Edmund said. "It's not my job to fix the bloody computers. That's four days now. I didn't stand for this in the carpet world, so I'll not stand for it here. Arrange for new contractors, immediately."

"Yes, sir," she said. "One more thing. It's top priority. Head office has left several confidential messages. They need you to contact them as a matter of urgency. They insist it must be your first action point for the morning."

Despite being late, Edmund paused to enjoy a warm smirk. He hadn't expected the invite for promotion to come so soon, although, who could blame them? They needed a good captain to steady the ship. Things must be desperate, he thought.

"The first rule in a negotiation, my Janet, never undress when she is already on all fours with her undercrackers round her ankles. Let her wet her own lips. I'll return the call *after* my morning duties."

"But, sir. They've left multiple messages. They said it's urgen-"

"Janet!" he scolded. "I'm not a simpleton. I didn't make it to where I am by squirting my load at the first whiff of quim. They can come to me... Now, that will be all. Off with you."

His Janet bowed and left. Edmund went straight to the A-suite. Thirty of the site's weakest Subs were sitting at their desks, Halos in place, The Woodland Parable midway through. He took his Block from Ms. Young (bee stings for tits and a miserable arse, but still worth a hard spaffle).

He'd memorised the instructions. The Subs would receive their dosage each morning for two weeks. All their lessons would take place in the A-suite, with the supervision of one teacher to administer the control commands when necessary. All work completed by each client would be recorded at the end of each day for comprehensive data collection and analysis. Edmund wanted to be the one who pressed the button to begin it all. He should have been the one on the broadcast yesterday. It should have been his site. Instead, they opted for that ridiculous woman and her thug nephew. Dr. Vaneman needed to take responsibility. Quite frankly, the catastrophe served him right.

Edmund looked at the thirty miniature red bodies on his Block's screen. He nodded at Ms. Young to turn off the touchwall, clearing their vision. Then he pressed the button to activate and watched as his palm glowed green. How lucky they were, Edmund thought, standing on the shoulders of the righteous to lift their noses above their own filth.

The Subs stood up in unison and roared. It was the most terrifying thing Edmund had ever experienced. He only had enough time to wet himself and curl up into a ball, before the frothing animals surrounded him. His skull was stamped against the floor (Industrial Grey Steel Tiling supplied at almost cost price). The last thing he saw before being knocked unconscious, was his vilest Sub, Abdul, smashing his Block into pieces.

23

BRUNO

Bruno was incapable of comprehending the inescapable weight of consequences being processed by the people he had disturbed through the night. He paid no attention to the sadness, the fear, the anger, the pain, the disgust. Bruno did not care because he was enjoying the greatest night of his short life, *and*, because Bruno is a dog.

He had briefly joined a band of howling strays, humping and sniffing each other as they routed through the CAPE station bins, just as a young man was escorted through the gates. The young man's aunt, having forgotten her solemn promise to get the best care for a broken client, was trying to stifle his nan's wailing as a Crusader dragged their boy to the floor.

Bruno had bounded across the rolling mounds of the landfill, dodging the desperate grabs of any litter hunters hoping to snag themselves a companion on their lonely rummage through the detritus.

He had dug up the pots of flowers surrounding the front door of a family home rupturing with anguish, as they raged and screamed and sobbed and begged, because a silly girl's 'lies' had led to them receiving notice for relocation.

He had stopped to take a dump on the unimpressive garden of an unimpressive house, as a man bedded down on his sofa and relaxed into a pill-induced haze. The man was blithely contemplating another few months of well-earned rest thanks to his newly braced leg, having spent the evening leaving voice messages for his ex-wife, telling her of his vindication.

Bruno had nuzzled into a broken client's mangled hand, hanging limply over her father's cradled embrace as he carried her home, barred from entering the A&E facility because her allowance wouldn't cover the required care. The mother followed silently, knowing, if her beautiful daughter were to die, she would choose to join her rather than stay with her husband.

He had sneaked into the back of an open van and consumed an entire tray of minced chicken canapes before being chased away by a band of traders in old-fashioned garb trying to set up the Plaza's food market, blissfully unaware that unwanted animals caught in the village were immediately destroyed.

And, by morning, he found his way to Zone 97's main road, twenty miles south of the concrete yard he had escaped from the day before. He pounced over potholes and through sprouting grass, snapping at butterflies, and dodging grey buses – his tale a wagging whirlwind of pure joy.

The contact was sudden, the car's back tyre crunching over Bruno's ribs in an instant. Before everything dulled to darkness, a hand jabbed at his stomach then grabbed his hind legs, trailing his tongue through the dirt as he was dragged under a hedge.

Bruno hadn't wasted an iota of thought on anything other than the instant gratification of eating, and rutting, and running, and howling, and smearing his nose in the sweet dregs clogging the gutters on that wonderful night. The everchanging sounds of misery that had permeated his playground were fleeting footnotes, the tragedy of lives merely an ambience to his grand adventure. Bruno did not care about any of them.

Because Bruno was a dog.

AUTHOR BIO

P.J. Willett is a British born author based in Birmingham. He has been a teacher of Drama, English, and Maths for fifteen years and has written columns for a variety of sports publications for a number of years. The Controlled is his debut novel – inspired by his years attending and teaching in deprived schools, and his love of science fiction and horror.

Printed in Great Britain
by Amazon

82053188R00150